CW01019610

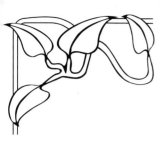
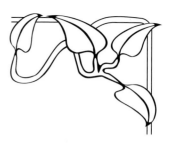

MISS

The memoirs of a young lady of quality
containing recollections of boarding school
discipline and intimate details of her chastisement

Translated from the French of
Miss Sadie Blackeyes

AKS
BOOKS
LIMITED

First published 1912
This Edition © 2002 by AKS Books Ltd.
PO Box 39, Bexhill-on-Sea,
East Sussex, England, TN40 1WR

Also published by AKS Books:

THE ART OF DISCIPLINE
THE ART OF DISCIPLINE VOLUME TWO
A HISTORY OF THE ROD
THE WAND OF VENUS
EXPERIENCES OF FLAGELLATION
A PERFECT MISTRESS
ACROSS MY LADY'S KNEE
THE QUEEN OF THE GROVE
THE LOST BREECHES
CHÂTEAU SOUMISSION
OUCH!!
THE SONG OF THE CANE
THE WHIP AND THE ROD
THE KISS OF THE WHIP
TALES OF THE UNBREECHED
SWEET RETRIBUTION
LINTON ABBEY
TROUBLE AT LINTON ABBEY
IN FRONT OF THE GIRLS
THE SATURDAY AFTERNOON DETENTION
SENT FOR SIX OF THE BEST
THE SCHOOL RECORD
THE CANE THAT LOST ITS STING
and
THE GOVERNESS COMPENDIUM

A catalogue record for this book is available from the British Library.

ISBN 1 899861 22 X
Designed in Great Britain.
Printed and bound by Antony Rowe Ltd.,
Chippenham, Wiltshire.

The recollections that are here written down are taken from real life. They are the memoirs of a well-brought up girl confined in a reformatory, who relates in a pleasant manner the incidents of her boarding-house life, incidents chiefly bearing on the mode of chastisement as practised by the directress.

As befitting, the names only have been changed by the author of this book, a charming young lady who has published her confessions under the name of Miss Sadie Blackeyes, an intimate friend of hers.

Sadie Blackeyes, who is herself a charming lady, uniting a most pretty face to the attraction of a keen intellect, has acted as heroine for the readers and the public. She has brought to this work a literary talent, not to embellish, but on the contrary to polish the prose, at times too undisciplined of a young girl, prose which the fine intellect of the past centuries would not have disowned at that epoch when bashfulness was to be found less in words than in acts.

Without having the brutal frankness of a Tallement de Reaux, nor the elegant wantonness of a Voltaire or of a Mirabeau, without the purity of style of these masters, let us say that the heroine of these memoirs nevertheless, says what she wishes to say, and in language sufficiently refined not to shock the decorum and the propriety of our times.

The pages that follow are sprightly, witty and of a gaiety natural to a young girl who is somewhat undisciplined, and even her Americanisms have not wholly estranged her from the books and classic culture of her race.

I

WHEN MY PARENTS forced me to enter a reformatory at X——, a small village close to Bruges in Flanders, I was a young girl sixteen-years of age.

Physically I was pretty, a fact I knew through the number of flirts I had had; and besides, my mirror showed me a young girl, slim and healthy, very Parisian in chic, notwithstanding an entirely English physical education.

My face—I have really no need to be modest—is prettily oval; the forehead and the eyes slightly elongated like the Orientals, curving gently beneath a mass of abundant dark auburn hair.

If you are an artist, retrace the portrait on a pastel, and inscribe on the frame the name of the model, as is customary: Lucette Jacqueline de Beaupré de Hêtraie.

This said, not to revert to the delicate subject of a description of my charms, be it known that my family belonged to the oldest nobility of Touraine; and at the time of the League, a Beaupré de Hêtraie had established for himself a sound reputation for gallantry, in debauching a dozen pretty Huguenots, that the hazards of pillage had thrown in his bed.

Another Beaupré de Hêtraie, if one believes Pierre de l'Estoile, had been in the intimate graces of Henri III de Valois, in the same manner as had been his friends Monsieur de Saint Luc de Caylius and Schonberg.

Let me be forgiven this short exposition of family history, but is it not extraordinary that a young girl as well born should have been the heroine of adventures absolutely authentic, which I shall relate with all the frankness of style that begot a queen of France a literary reputation with which I have no desire to vie.

My father, at the time that the recital of these adventures begins, was a country gentleman living midst his dogs and horses in the manner of those apoplectic old gentlemen which one sees on the English prints of Cecil Alden.

My mother had died when as a very small girl I still had great need of her tender protection, for she had been a sweet sentimental creature, confined to her home, bestowing little time upon the contingencies of daily life, much inclined to the exquisite reveries of the most romantic of the poets.

My father, on the death of my mother, kept me with him, and brought me up not too strictly, that is to say, he made me his confidant in his hopes for the return of the old régime, taught me to ride a horse and to jump a hedge, and gave me that freedom of behaviour which was the cause of all my vexations when the period of the seven lean cows followed that of the seven fat cows.

The day the stranger brought misfortune into my father's château coincided with my fifteenth birthday.

This stranger was a governess, tall, and not at all disagreeable to look at physically.

My father fell in love with her, to the point of neglecting his daily occupations and his best friends, such as M. de Rombobinet, master of the wolf-hunt.

The marriage took place, and from that day life at the château became unbearable for me.

My stepmother, who, up to the day that made her mistress of the château, had shown herself of amiable disposition, changed overnight, and embittered herself against me, partly because I resisted her, partly because my aristocratic ancestry made her conscious of her having usurped in the château a place which was not hers.

My father did not defend me. When crazy with rage and grief, I used to seek his support and consolation, he would close his ears and shut himself up in his study.

His weakness of character prevented him from siding with either the one or the other; after the fashion of many men, he left to chance the care of settling matters for the best or for the worse.

This behaviour hastened events, and to be brief, as the purpose of this confession is not to portray my family life, but the three painful years that I spent in the most infernal gaol where one can confine a young girl, especially a young girl well brought up.

The disputes with my stepmother were so frequent that I evaded her as much as possible. It was at table only that quiet was to be found, for my father exacted to be left undisturbed while he dined, as one who shares the ideas of the celebrated Brillat-Savarin.

All that I did, my stepmother took as a pretext for unending wrangling, whereby all the vulgarity of her character was freely made manifest.

"Lucette, behave yourself, I dislike your tomboy manners which are in bad taste and which I will not tolerate in my house."

Those words "in my house" would send me into a rage that I had difficulty in mastering. She would not hesitate to make uncivil remarks about me in front of my friends.

I can remember a Thursday when Marthe Ribier, the daughter of my father's solicitor, a silly girl in her 'teens, was on a visit at my stepmother's.

I was serving the tea, and as I approached Mme. Ribier to offer her a cup of tea, I slipped, with the result that the dress of the venerable lady was inundated.

"You are stupid," said my stepmother, "leave everything and go to your room."

And as I refused, haughtily silent, but not with anger.

"Go up to your room; I promise you that if you do not obey me, I shall have no scruple in giving you a spanking."

It is impossible to describe the state of mind I was in, the shame that this awful threat caused me.

Alone with my stepmother I would have replied saucily.

But this threat in front of Mme. Ribier and her daughter, who was smiling foolishly, left me helpless.

Tears welled up to my eyes, and setting down the cup of tea, I left the drawing-room, abashed and as red as a peony.

It was the first time in my life that I was threatened by that vulgar word "spanking."

Naturally as a small child, my nurse and my mother had spanked me two or three times... I was then only a child four- or five-years old.

But now, a big girl fifteen-years old, I was threatened by this ignoble chastisement in the presence of a lady and her daughter.

In my room, where I lay sobbing with rage and pain, the horrid word buzzed in my ears like an obsession.

"Spanking, spanking, I will give you a spanking." It was the precise meaning of the word that disgusted me, the exact designation of that part of my body on which the stupid and shameful punishment was to be applied.

My stepmother had noticed my unhappiness, and from that day would look at me spitefully with a smile that left me trembling between the wish to cry and the wish to strangle the odious creature.

For a trifle, a broken vase, that was followed by a violent altercation, she told me another time: "Understand, Lucette, that you must not provoke me beyond endurance, for I am quite capable of granting you that which I once promised to do!"

A hot flush rose to my face. I could only stammer: "You, you, you would do that... You would dare to do that?"

She came near me and tried to bend me shamefully against her; but I was big and strong, and she perceived at once that she could never accomplish her infamous idea.

She let me go, and as I disengaged myself, she slapped me with all her strength on both my cheeks.

I stood stunned, sobbing; she profited by my hesitation to leave the room and, as I threw myself against the door to scratch the worthless woman, she was already on the landing and had locked me in my own room.

I writhed on my bed, biting my pillow, tearing the lace of my coverlet, and thoughts of vengeance most atrocious and absurd crossed my brain like lightning in a stormy sky.

Nevertheless, although ignorant of the reasons that poison the life of certain people, I did not doubt but that my stepmother had some deep reason to hate me thus.

I believe that had it been in her power to make me disappear for good from earth, she would have done so without hesitating, to such a degree was my presence in my father's château odious to her.

One night as I was going up to my room, which was in the right wing of the château, I heard a violent discussion that seemed to come from my father's study.

I leaned over my balcony and noticed that the study was lit; the window had been left open, as we were in the month of June and the atmosphere was warm and sultry.

"I tell you that it is impossible to manage the little minx, it is impossible to keep her here, life is no longer bearable because of her, and besides... I foresee a fine scandal one of these days... the hussy flirts over much, and from what I overheard in the servants talk, there is just time to prevent harm happening, if it has not yet happened."

This is what I heard, paler than a corpse, waiting, my heart beating loudly, to hear my father's answer... my father did not reply... he did not get up to strangle that woman, he raised no protest to avenge his daughter thus odiously calumniated.

From my window I could see him walk to and fro in his study, his back bent, his hands on his ears.

"Do what you like... do what you like, but by Jove, leave me in peace... yes, yes, I'll write... there... are you content?"

He had sat down, and taking his fountain-pen from his pocket, he was writing, stopping every now and then, seeming to wait for the sentences that his wife dictated to him.

The letter finished, he sealed it and gave it to his wife.

And then silence followed, and my father called his two basset-hounds, and I saw him going along the road that spread out all white into the blue night.

I had not well understood this scene, but fear prevented me from sleeping, for I did not doubt but that my stepmother had again committed some infamous act.

Not for a moment did the thought of going to a boarding-house touch my mind, and my faculties lead to this one thought; my stepmother wanted to whip me, and doubtless, she sought means to realise this threat.

I was expecting some such aggression to such an extent, that I had bought a small Italian stiletto that I carried with me, resolved to use all means in order not to submit to that degrading punishment.

Besides, I would leave my room only to saddle my pony and escape as far as possible into the forest.

The elementary education of the former governess did not enable her to ride a horse and thus I was certain that she would not impose her odious society upon me.

Nevertheless, like the flat calms that precede the most awful storms, the unnatural quiet that I had enjoyed for many weeks had only hastened the approaching storm.

One morning I was awakened with a start by the grating of the lock of my door. I am a little bit nervous and the slightest sound is enough to waken me from deep slumber. My eyes still troubled with sleep, I nevertheless recognised the silhouette of my stepmother.

She in my room! At such an early hour! It was enough to make me feel on my guard. I sat up and watched my enemy as she approached.

Deception was portrayed on the face of the shrew. I believe that she did not think me so wide awake, and my resolute attitude seemed to baffle all her previsions.

"Lucette, I want to tell you, for I do not wish to create a scandal in front of the servants, that I mean to punish you for the insolence and the spitefulness you display towards me. I shall not be severe; submit therefore to the small punishment that I shall inflict upon you. I thought that in this room... nothing easier... you undressed... everything allows for discretion, and you will be spared the painful turning up of your

dresses that would have been necessary had you been dressed...
be docile... I will not whip you hard."

I am sure that at these words my eyes must have been
staring out of my head. I was choking and could only reply in a tone
of absolute bewilderment. "But you are mad ! What do you mean?"

"I say," repeated my stepmother, and her eyes suddenly
shone with an evil light that transfigured her, "I say that you *will*
be spanked, and like a little child. I want to break your pride. Do
you think yourself such a big girl that I dare not lift your skirts
and untie your drawers? The punishment that is inflicted on
small, undisciplined children will break down your infernal
impudence, I wish you to be submissive to the point of kissing
the hand that will have spanked you! What will you say of the
gesture?... Be reasonable, lie flat on your stomach and submit to
your punishment... Later you will thank me!"

When a girl is fifteen-years-old she does not like being
treated like a small child, especially when these words are used
as a pretext for the most ignoble of corporal punishments.

I *was* fifteen-years-old and of good birth, and these two
things made the blood rush through my veins, and as my
stepmother approached to uncover the bedclothes and expose
my nudity, I slapped her with all my strength, unable to master
my violence.

This quick gesture plunged me into crazy anguish...
What would happen, what would be the consequence of my
act?... The thoughts whirled in my brain, with a speed that my
pen cannot trace.

That which happened... was that my stepmother left
the room threatening me with her finger, her eyes full of hate,
meeting mine.

This look, a presage of a struggle without pity, plunged
me into despair.

"Good God ! Good God ! What have I done? I am
nevertheless not wicked... Oh, how unhappy I am!"

And I wept, I wept away all the tears of my poor little
heart, in a fit of despairing sadness.

The result of the scene was made apparent the day after.

Without any preliminaries and with an evil joy, my stepmother told me that I was to leave for a reformatory in Belgium until of age.

As I sobbed in the grip of a child's big grief, she added in a honeyed voice:

"Do not cry Lucette, there as here, you will always be Mademoiselle de Hêtraie."

"It is not a vulgar place where proximity and too large a number of boarders would have merely allowed your bad habits to develop… You will get on very well there, the directress is one of my friends and you will be treated accordingly."

I threw myself at my father's feet, begging him to intercede for me, supplicating, promising to do whatever was asked of me… I think that if at that moment my stepmother had given me the alternative between leaving and staying, and yet the conditions of receiving the promised chastisement, I would have chosen to stay.

But already the carriage was loaded with my trunks, and it was my stepmother herself who conducted me there… beyond all hope… beyond the free life.

I shall always remember that unlucky day; I was dressed in a dark blue walking-skirt and a white blouse, and a big cloak to protect me…. It was thus that I arrived at Brussels.

In the town, my stepmother bought the rest of my clothes; and the clothes for the boarding school were so elegant that I was delighted, for I should be lying if I did not count coquettishness amongst my shortcomings.

From Brussels we took the train that goes to Bruges, the Home for the Education of Young Undisciplined Girls of which I speak being in the country, between this city and the Dutch frontier.

The landscape interested me; the old dead city built along the sombre canals diverted my attention and put me into a reverie. I inherited this characteristic from my poor mother and while following the movements of the big swans dedicated to Marguerite de Bourgogne, I forgot to think of the aim of my voyage.

The small tram-car that passes in front of the railway

station carried us through the town and we were soon in the country, with nothing on the horizon but some idle windmills, their arms like the Roman cross.

At eight o'clock in the evening, I got down with my stepmother in front of a large garden, at the other end of which one could make out buildings in red brick.

Now I am a lady; fifteen-years have elapsed since the day that I first crossed the threshold of the reformatory, and yet, I feel oppressed with grief when I remember the anguish of the hour when the heavy bronze door turned on its hinges to receive my stepmother and the poor little girl that I was then.

At the end of a walk lined with plane trees, the central wing of a large building in the style of Louis XIV loomed up.

Apprised of our arrival by a bell, the President came down the steps to meet my stepmother.

Of this first encounter with her who was the evil genius throughout my life, who fashioned my poor little soul to the point of making me a cowardly and cringing thing, I shall always keep a clear recollection.

From the moment that I was in the presence of this lady whose name was Madame Evangeline de Quirinodo, and who, it was affirmed, had once been a nun who had renounced her vows, from that moment I feared a danger more terrifying and more vague than any physical punishment, and which my virginal innocence could not define.

Mme. Evangeline de Quirinodo was a tall woman with red hair, of that mahogany red that had made famous the tresses of the women of the Rialto; her face was impassive, strikingly pale except for the redness of the lips, well marked and so swollen with blood, that they looked like fresh wounds.

The elegance of her figure was emphasised by the irreproachable cut of a tight blue skirt; a blouse in Malines lace compressed the firm treasure of her bosom, a surprisingly young bosom for a woman thirty-years-old, for the firmness of her breasts was revealed beneath the flimsy lace pattern.

"This is your little girl !" she simply said, nodding towards me.

Her voice crept into my ears with a mildness that attenuated a little bit the feeling of fear that this strange and, more than beautiful woman, caused me.

I had seen in my father's library, a drawing by Rops that had revealed to me, certain things without explaining them.

Mme. de Quirinodo had the same face, the eyes circled by shadows and consumed by I could not say what sort of dark musings.

Intelligence, poison and a malignant will-power issued from these eyes, and their attraction reminded me of a poor little bird hypnotised by the golden eyes of a serpent of India.

"I think, Madame, that we better leave this child by herself for a little, it is not sensible that she should hear what you may have to say to me concerning her faults, her vices and her virtues… for I expect that she has virtues."

The red arch of her mouth unbent in a smile, revealing small and sharp white teeth.

She rang a bell. A servant, coquettishly dressed, took me away, while the directress and my stepmother discussed the question of my internment.

Without saying a word, the servant lead me to the parlour which was furnished in English style. A collection of cakes and tea was set on a small table. I am greedy, and the smell of hot buns triumphing over my anguish, I began to eat heartily.

The servant asked me with a smile: "Are you the new boarder?"

Lifting my eyes I saw a pretty girl, fair and plump, and her gracefulness gave me confidence. "Yes, I am the new boarder… Is life hard here?"

She smiled again, shrugged her shoulders and contented herself with replying: "Good God, yes… but one gets accustomed to it, and there are a few compensations that make it worthwhile!"

My meal ended, she cleared up the things and left me alone with my thoughts. They were not complex ones; the surprise of the new conditions around me did not allow me to classify my feelings. I stayed quite an hour contemplating the prints that hung on the wall, depicting portraits of women of the English school.

The door opening suddenly made me jump in my chair; it was Mme. de Quirinodo herself who came towards me in a gentle rustling of her long dress.

She tapped me on the cheek. "Well my child, my little Lucette, you are now one of us, I hope you shall be obedient and submissive; there, don't cry, we shall talk of that later, come and say good-bye to your stepmother!"

I followed her, my head bent down, hardly able to keep back the tears that welled up to my swollen eyes, unwilling to show my grief to my stepmother.

The good-byes were cold, hers as well as mine, but nevertheless, when the gate closed on her who represented for me all the past of my happy life, I could not master my tears any longer, and began to cry, and to cry, to cry away all the big chagrin that filled my heart with bitterness.

"Now then, come Lucette, I shall show you your room… you will not be uncomfortable, and if you follow my advice… carefully, you will leave this place wholly transformed… later on you will remember and be grateful to the discipline that changes a young girl, turbulent and vicious, into an angel, pure and gentle."

At the end of this short speech, to which I could find nothing to reply, Mme. de Quirinodo lead me to the right wing of the building allocated as living rooms to the students.

We reached a long corridor opening into twenty-four doors, twelve on each side. I noticed that all these doors were locked from the outside.

Mme. de Quirinodo, who now preceded me, opened one of the doors and I entered a small room, really much more cosy than I expected.

A thick pale green carpet covered the floor, and the walls were painted in white varnish. The furniture consisted of a small iron bedstead, a desk, a wardrobe, a looking-glass, two chairs, an arm chair and a wash-stand with a toilet-seat. It was perfect for a little recluse, and I was agreeably surprised, as I had imagined myself lodged in a narrow cell, on a poor folding bedstead with nothing but a mug of water and a piece of dry black bread.

"This is your room, Lucette," said Mme. de Quirinodo. "I hope you will live in it always and that you will not change it for the prison cell—it depends entirely on you! All your companions, who number twenty-four, have similar rooms... and at night the Dean locks each girl in her room, for we want no disorder whatever... you understand me? If you are in need of anything, the bell at the head of the bed informs the Dean, who comes to see what is the matter."

"I shall now give you a summary of the rules and the organisation of this house that I have the honour to direct."

"As regards studies, the programme is that of a high school."

"There are three classes, the youngest between eight- and twelve-years of age, then those between thirteen and fifteen, and the big girls between fifteen and eighteen.

"All depends on the attainments of the students, as for instance Alice de Digue, who, although only fourteen-years-old, is in the class of the big girls!"

While showing me the dancing-room, the refectory, the studies, *etc.*, Mme. de Quirinodo questioned me about the list of my studies.

"Yes, you are sufficiently instructed, you will take your classes with the big girls... you will find amongst them several young day-scholars with whom I forbid you to speak... for you are in the denomination of a disciplinary, while the day students are here merely to follow the classes of our teachers."

"I have no responsibility whatever as to their conduct, but it is a different matter as regards my boarders whom I must rule with a firm hand."

"I will shortly introduce you to your companions, those who are here for the same reasons as you are... for the present I shall ask you to put on the uniform of the boarders... It has been cut to your measurement, and I hope it will suit you."

She opened the wardrobe and took out a dress of grey

cloth, a grey quite handsome.

"Here you are, would you like to try it on?"

"But… Madame!"

I did not move, slightly embarrassed to undress in front of her. She frowned and looked at me straight in the eyes.

I did not hesitate any longer and undressed, that is to say I took off my blouse and skirt to put on the new clothes that she held out to me.

The dress was a simple walking-skirt cut with good taste, a chemisette in grey flannel but of a lighter grey served for a blouse, a stiff collar and a blue and red tie completed the house-dress.

I looked at myself in the looking-glass and, thus clothed, I was very pretty.

The President, perceiving my coquettishness, contented herself with saying:

"You are right in liking pretty dresses, and good taste in knowing how to dress is part of the beauty of a woman, and I am intransigent in all that concerns care in dress, even the most intimate… you have your complete outfit and you must have been able to judge how particular I am as regards the elegance of under-clothing… now Lucette, follow me that I may introduce you to your playmates."

We went down into the garden where on a big lawn some twenty girls were playing joyfully under the surveillance of the Dean.

Mme. de Quirinodo took a whistle, and quiet superseded as by enchantment, and while the Dean came towards us, the pupils fell in line in an attitude of deference and submission that could not but make me wonder a little.

The President introduced me to begin with to the Dean.

"This is our new pupil, Mlle. Lucette de Hêtraie, she is difficult to manage but I hope she will improve," and turning towards me: "Lucette, I request that you obey Miss Elisa, your teacher. I hope that your conduct will always be above reproach and will merit no punishment." The sub-directress smiled equivocally and this I disliked.

She was a tall and large woman in her thirties, dark and pretty, of a severe type of beauty, a little like those heads of Minerva used as emblematic of the Republic.

She was dressed in black, simply and in good taste, but such as she appeared to me, I disliked her, for she inspired in me an unreasoned fear, which the story that follows was nevertheless to justify.

My playmates were all pretty girls; there were amongst this charming swarm, little girls between eight- and ten-years of age, and adolescents, and girls of eighteen nearing womanhood.

Submission, a servile submission, was depicted on all the lovely faces; it needed but a look from Mme. de Quirinodo or a gesture from the Dean to upset them.

The introductions were over just as playtime came to an end.

The students separated into three groups under the command of a teacher.

Mme. de Quirinodo put me in the class of the big girls

that comprised eight young girls between fifteen- and eighteen-years of age. Miss Elisa was the teacher of this group.

The rôle of each teacher was merely one of surveillance and discipline. The lessons were given by professors of the town, and the classes consisted of day-students as well as boarders, who came from Bruges, and neighbouring resorts, and showed in no way the effects of the extremist discipline that reigned over the boarders of Mme. de Quirinodo.

These young girls, even though of high-birth, were looked down upon with ironic contempt by the day-students, and this was not the least of the obloquies of the régimen of the reformatory, to have to be threatened and to have to undergo humiliatory chastisement in the presence of these young girls, who they themselves were sheltered from such procedures. I shall describe briefly the way in which the reformatory functioned, so as not to revert to tiresome details which only encumber the most interesting part of my confessions.

The class, that is to say group A, to which I belonged, was composed of eight boarders and a dozen of day-students.

The school rooms were in a pretty building at the other end of the garden, and quite separated from the buildings, study-rooms, dormitories, *etc…* reserved for our usage, to us poor so-called shabby sheep, removed from life, most often victims of family rancour.

I can assert that amongst the boarders, except for seven or eight young pupils that were really perverse, the others were good and sweet girls, culpable of having inconvenienced by their presence certain filth which even good families are not always screened from.

This was my case as well as that of Georgette Schrive, a young girl seventeen-years-old, who straightaway became my companion, my friend, in the most caressing and the most feminine sense of the word. She was a handsome blonde, with a porcelain complexion, lovely as an eighteenth-century pastel. Tall and well-built like a woman past her twenties, she was a lovely thing, and withall, intelligent and sweet.

From the day that we met, our hearts joined in

harmony in a silent vow of loyal friendship.

We were not allowed to converse much together and although I saw in the eyes and in the attitude of my companion that she had many disclosures to make on the régime of the reformatory, she was unable to warn me of the troubles and calamities of which I was to become a piteous victim.

Nevertheless at the end of our afternoon classes when I had felt the blush of indignation rush to my cheeks at the mocking looks of the day-students, as we strolled beneath an aisle of plane-trees before the evening meal, we managed to tell each other the anxieties of our young hearts.

Georgette looked at me with tenderness, and as we walked silently along she circled my waist with her left arm, and hip against hip she made me gently confess to her, with kind childish words of consolation.

"Poor little kitten, whatever did you do to be imprisoned in this inferno?"

Lifting my eyes towards her I told her my story.

She listened silently, nodding her pretty fair head.

"Just like me, my poor little Lulu! I had a stepmother... the same story... just imagine, little puss, that, that odious woman once beat me unmercifully with a whip. I shall never forget that day; it was in the morning and I was dressing in front of the looking-glass. The day before I had had a serious dispute with her and no one to defend me, for I have no father. Briefly, she came up behind me like a fury and without saying a word she began to lash me on the hips, the shoulders and the arms with a rattan whip.

I had a petticoat on, my bosom and arms were bare, you can imagine how terrible the pain was. I writhed on the bed, and the shrew whipped my legs, my thighs, and all that she could reach... I am proud, my little Lulu, and yet I must confess it, I knelt before her... and I asked her pardon... only, the next day I revenged myself by trying to poison her... yes... I was crazy...

now that I know, that which I know, I understand it would have
been better to have borne the whipping that I got at home; it
was still less painful and above all less shameful than that which
one has to bear here."

She sighed, and anxiety widened my pupils, seeking
details of this life of discipline, the fear of which almost made
me crazy.

I had not spoken to Georgette of my stepmother's threats
and of her desire to whip me; this had seemed to me indecent to
relate, and I had passed over this incident without a word.

Now Georgette's confession revived my anguish, and I
could not help thinking through association of ideas, that this
ignoble punishment that I had been threatened with at home,
could very possibly be realised here.

"But," I asked timidly, "how do they punish the
culpable pupils; it is terrible not to know, and I have such
terrible apprehensions!"

"Oh! My little darling, it is always too soon to become
acquainted with sorrow. I shall tell you nothing... and moreover,
you will soon learn the truth, and in undergoing the sad
experience yourself."

"Nevertheless Mme. de Quirinodo does not appear to
me wicked... do you think she would go as far as to thrash
young girls? Big young girls!"

"Hush, my kitty! Do not speak so loudly, if they heard
us it would not be long before you would find out how they act
in this ignoble gaol."

"But tell me, I beg you, my dear Georgette!"

"Poor darling, the word alone would make you blush as
it made me blush when I first came here three-years ago."

"I know," I said in abashed and halting voice, "they
punish the big girls as they do small babies... then if Mme. de
Quirinodo were to hear us..."

"Well," replied Georgette, bending down her head,
"we would both of us be whipped."

Eight days sufficed to accustom myself to my
surroundings and get in touch with my new playmates.

Now that I was informed of the mode of punishment used in the reformatory, I lived in a continual nervous tension.

Consequently I was of exemplary behaviour, and of docility such that my schoolmistress, Miss Elisa, could not but be satisfied.

The mistrust that I cherished against her disappeared little by little, and I ventured to flatter myself that she sympathised with me, this making her more indulgent towards me than towards the others. In fact, she was playing with me as a cat plays with a mouse.

I shall always remember the end of an afternoon when I first came into contact—this time only as a witness—with the coercive practices of the reformatory.

It was eight days after my arrival, more or less the first day that I had lived like my other companions, the preceding days having been for me days of trying on of the school clothes, confession, for it is necessary that I should say that the boarding-house was very religious, and that a Pastor and a priest were specially attached to it. The end of this day was noticeable for a warm and overwhelming temperature. Through the open windows the twittering of birds disturbed us, and more than one inattentive little head turned towards the foliage that scented the air with a languorous perfume. Pen in mouth, I watched a big blackbird sporting on a branch; my right hand neighbour, Germaine, a small plump brunette, lovely as can be, followed it also with deplorable attention. The movements of the bird were so funny that the young girl gave a sudden laugh, which resounded in the quiet room like the pure sound of tinkling crystal.

I turned to her; instantly the poor little thing had changed her charming and frolicsome visage into a frowning and severe one, and her eyes, looking upwards beneath her long curved eyelashes, seemed to supplicate the superb school-mistress, whose countenance had taken on an expression of wicked harshness.

"Well!… is it you, Germaine, who dare allow yourself such manners?… Do you know that each day you are becoming more and more impudent. I believe it is necessary that you learn you are not here to laugh and to enjoy yourself but to learn subjection. You hear me!... and I shall bend the most undisciplined character as I do this rod."

She took hold of a pliant cane and getting up she twisted it angrily between her hands.

"Get up and come here."

Germaine had got up, and with bent head, her chin trembling as though she were about to cry, she went towards the platform from where Miss Elisa towered over her pupils.

"Get up... come near me, come on, nearer still."

Germaine, her elbow raised, made a slight parrying movement, but *pif, paf*, the stiff hand slapped the round cheeks of the young girl, who began to cry gently.

I was indignant. Germaine was sixteen-years-old and the slaps she had just received constituted for me an outrageous affront, as though I myself had received them.

I had not overcome my surprise and my anger, and all my feelings were in revolt, for at that time I had not yet acquired that submission which rods and sticks later undertook to obtain.

"This time," continued the implacable voice of Miss Elisa, "this time you will receive twenty-four lashes with a cane, only I shall turn you towards these young ladies so that the new girl be a witness of your shameful punishment... get ready!"

There could no longer be any doubt as to the meaning of her words; the dreadful "thing" was about to happen, and in my indignation I was on the point of forgetting that it would be worse, had the authoritative schoolmistress ordered me to take the place of Germaine.

Poor young girl, how I pitied her; my heart ached for her and the agitation of my small breasts, round and firm, betrayed the emotion that dominated my nerves.

With awkward movements, her eyes beseeching and her mouth puckered in an adorable pout, Germaine obeyed Miss Elisa, who had told her to make herself ready.

And I followed with my eyes the indecent preparations that were expected of her. The hands of the young girl had lifted up on each side the grey skirt, disclosing small high-heeled

shoes, light grey stockings that moulded the curves of her calves... Trembling, she tried to untie the knot of her drawers, smart and chaste, dysloc whose lace fell in a sort of froth over her knees, bashfully pressed one against the other.

"Stop your mimics, Miss, it is not the first time that you are showing your posterior in public. If you cannot find the knot I shall help you to do so and you'll see what you'll get on your fat backside."

That is what I heard and did not move, for I was afraid, and the awful hold that the flagellation had over my brain already acted on my senses.

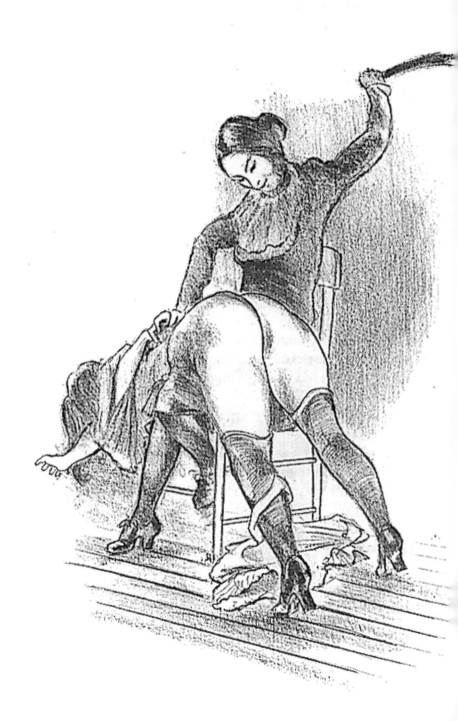

My companions on the other hand afforded a curious spectacle. On the mobile faces of these young girls the feelings that agitated them were clearly depicted... No trace of pity in the beautiful eyes levelled on the victim, and the blush that spread over the cheeks and the forehead of my companions was the afflux of blood caused by evil desires.

Germaine had untied the ribbons of her drawers and the light garment fell about her ankles. She was standing in front of her school-mistress in an attitude in which fear had overcome the bashfulness of the young girl.

Miss Elisa turned her chair around and sitting down comfortably, her knees slightly apart, she took hold of Germaine by her arm and drew her towards herself.

She took a rod that was hooked under the desk and I shall never forget the impression I had on seeing this long sheaf of pliant switches, and which I was later to feel the effects of, on my own flesh.

All this occurred more rapidly than I can write it down.

The docility of Germaine was moreover perfect, and it was without the slightest revolt that she bent down, resting on her stomach on the knees of the school-mistress.

Slowly, like a priest accomplishing some divine service, Miss Elisa lifted up the grey skirt and the petticoat that Germaine had let drop.

The chemise was lifted with a slowness that seemed to me an abyss of shame for Germaine.

And then... I could not refrain a little "Oh !" of offended modesty.

For the first time in my life, I was seeing the bottom of a young girl, and in such a posture that I could not turn aside my eyes from this charming object. Let me be forgiven but I have promised to be truthful, the impression made on my mind by the sight of Germaine's bottom was an impression most agreeable.

To undertake a description of what I saw is too improper for a young woman who still blushes as these recollections come back to her.

Nevertheless, to tell the truth, I had in front of me

framed in the white linen of her chemise and the folds of her skirt and petticoat, a large moon of white and sweet flesh, mysteriously separated by a deep groove that curved in between the thighs, into a dark shadow, guardian of a delightful mystery.

The stockings drawn up to the middle of the thighs revealed them round and elegantly slender, even though Germaine was a little plump.

This sight I shall remember always. Never had I seen a young girl, almost a woman, in an attitude so indecent, and the idea alone, that I could be put into a similar posture, covered my face with blushes of shame.

I was in the front row of desks. Thus seated, I was merely some two-yards from the backside of the culprit. Miss Elisa raised her right knee, hooking the heel of her high shoes to the crossbar of her chair. This movement threw into relief the roundness of the bottom which opened slightly showing up the amber-coloured depths of the middle slit of the juvenile planisphere.

"Once again you are ready to receive a spanking; you are and always will be an incorrigible little vermin... but this time I shall chastise your bottom in such a way that you won't forget it!"

Miss Elisa's voice bit like steel, and a shiver passed down my back, and this fear was not without a certain attraction, a mixture of sensuality and curiosity for a chastisement that would threaten me also some day.

II

THIS DISQUIETING temptation which makes us seek danger, handed me over already to the infamous punishment of the rod and the cat-o'-nine-tails; moved by the incomprehensible feelings that Edgar Poe calls the *demon of perversity*, I was to yield myself up and furnish the pretext that permitted my mistress the shameful lifting up of my skirts, the prelude of a whipping in front of my companions.

Miss Elisa raised her arm and I thought that I was going to scream, but fortunately no sound came from my contracted throat. She lifted her arm and the rod whistled in the stillness as it came down with a dull sound on the bottom that humbly offered itself.

The buttocks contracted at this brutal lash, hollowed out two small dimples in the white mass of flesh, the loins evading in a movement that tried to withdraw the buttocks to avoid the second blow that was coming.

Miss Elisa whipped slowly and thus each lash with the birch switches afforded its maximum of suffering... while the humiliating exhibition distracted all the more the pudicity of poor Germaine.

The rod fell again, and I saw the small pink streak that striped her buttocks transversely to the cleft that separated them.

Each time that the arm accomplished its tormenting work a scream more and more shrill replied to the dull sound of the switches probing into the soft flesh.

And Germaine's bottom danced madly now and widening and exaggerating the opening of its groove, revealing the pink and delicate line of her virginity.

My eyes dazed by the blood that coursed through my temples, through my heart, saw but the terrible rod descending without respite in a mad whirlwind.

Germaine was supplicating, and the humbleness of her pardons made me judge what must have been her suffering and her distraction... Pain intersected her phrases with sobs... The switches kept time to the childish words that the pretty little mouth addressed to the whipping teacher.

"Miss... enough... par... pardon... oh!... ooh! I shall never... never do it again! Mercy... you are tearing me... ooh... not there! not there!"

The indiscreet rod lashed anywhere, on the summit of the buttocks, between the half-opened globes where the feminine tenderness is so very painful, and there were howls of a child that twisted her loins, her beseeching hands that vainly tried to spread themselves out to protect the bottom, now all red, of a red that shone like a burn.

The sub-mistress was strong, she had no difficulty in maintaining the young girl in her sad position, even though the latter kicked in all directions not troubling about the indecency of these obligatory gymnastics.

As it had been Miss Elisa's intention to give "just a small whipping" to the too joyous Germaine, she had not taken the trouble of tying the culprit as was the custom for severer punishments.

The rod lashed the bottom of the poor darling at least twenty-five times, and those who have never been whipped should not misapprehend this number... twenty-five blows with a rod on a bare bottom is enough to make yell any lass whose bottom is so delicate and tender.

When Germaine was freed from the embrace that bent her over Miss Elisa's knees, her big bottom was red, giving the aspect of a beautiful dark peony.

The poor thing, heedless of her nudity, was rubbing her seat with the palms of her hands, twisting her legs one against the other, her shoulders quivering, agitated by convulsive sobs.

Miss Elisa, whose pinched face reflected a bizarre mixture of exaggerated Puritanism and of lust, called the attention of the suffering Germaine to her state.

"Will you pull up your drawers! Are you not ashamed

to stay in such a state in front of your companions?"

But my companions, as I found out later, were not in the least shocked by the exhibition of the chubby charms of their school-fellow. It was not for the first time that they were present at a similar spectacle; they all knew one another under this aspect and their adolescent bodies had no secrets to unveil.

I was therefore the only one to be moved by this sight and because of this, I was to my teacher and my companions an object of curiosity more interesting than poor Germaine, whose bottom they had seen an incalculable number of times.

During all the time that the whipping had lasted my companions and my teacher herself had observed me from the corner of their eyes, one of those long looks beneath the eyelashes, as is natural to a woman when she begins to become coquettish, deceitful and inquisitive as befitting a pretty young daughter of Eve.

Evidently, my psychological state troubled them and my presence increased for them the interest of a spectacle whose frequency alone had rendered commonplace.

What were my impressions at the sight of Germaine's nude bottom? What were the feelings of indignation that agitated my palpitating bosom? What was exactly the acuteness of my shame?

Their looks clearly indicated that they were asking themselves those questions, as I myself, a little later, tried to read with the same unhealthy curiosity that which was written on the face of a young and new spectator to this sort of punishment.

Germaine, having imprisoned her pretty round bottom in the fragile envelope of her drawers, stepped down from the platform and sat down on her bench, but not without repressing a small "aie!" of pain as her inflamed bottom came into contact with the hard bench.

Stealthily I observed her. She no longer appeared to suffer pain, and as one of her neighbours with a bold gesture ran her hand over the roundness of her buttocks, which her tight skirt exaggerated, I was surprised to note that Germaine answered her by a queer smile that made me pensive and agitated me.

This first whipping, of which I was a witness, opened my eyes a little bit... From that day physical beauty was revealed to me under its worst agitating aspect, and the poison coursed through my young veins, veins of a healthy and ardent young girl.

I had such agitating dreams the night following this small school punishment, that I woke up several times a prey to sensations whose persistence and whose preciseness plunged me into self-disgust. I did not refrain from gently alleviating myself in a way that my instinct alone of my nascent sensuality dictated to me.

The blue crows-feet that circled my eyes betrayed the following day the fatigue which I yet felt. Miss Elisa, entering my room while I was brushing my long auburn hair, did not mistake the languished look of my slightly pale countenance.

She looked at me with her dark eyes and I faltered at her look.

"Oh my little one! You verily need to be watched... I won't insist... but I can see by your embarrassment that you quite understand what I mean!"

"Miss! Good Heavens... no!" I stammered, distracted at the idea that this woman knew the cause of my sleepiness.

"Do not answer... I see that your stepmother had not made a mistake in particularly referring you to the President. I shall besides inform her as is my duty, of this shameful habit, far too general with young girls of your age!"

"I beg you, Miss... do not say anything... I do not know what you are thinking of... I swear that I have done nothing bad!"

"Dress yourself and do not reply... From today on, I warn you that I consider you sufficiently acquainted with the rules of the school to subject you to punishments that I inflict on your companions—may this warning suffice!"

At these words she turned gracefully on her heels and entered the adjoining room of my friend Georgette.

I heard her imperious voice apostrophising the poor young thing for some insignificant detail of dress.

"It's always the same thing... disorder in everything and everywhere—open your hand that I may apply twenty strokes with a rod."

I heard Georgette's voice stammering some vague and timid excuses, then the sharp sound of the cane on the palm of the poor girl.

Breathlessly I listened to the sound of the punishment. For sure it was less shameful than a whipping, but the pain was just as burning... in time I thought it would be better to be beaten on the bottom than on the palm of the hands... In the former case there is always a very special sensation that at times renders the punishment less disagreeable than one would imagine. I am speaking of course of mild whippings, for as regards real flagellation, the pain is so intense that one would not submit of one's own free will to such debasing commands.

Georgette bore her early morning punishment with sufficient courage; her screams and prayers broke out only after the fifteenth blow as her punishment was about to end.

As we went down to the refectory to take our breakfast, she passed by me and putting her hand on my cheek she smiled sadly as she said: "Feel how hot it is!"

"You are suffering dearie?"

I very gently kissed the reddened palm of the trembling little hand, and the touch of the female skin was enervating and sweet to my lips as the contact of a material of silk.

"Lucette?"

It's Georgette who calls me as she comes out of the refectory, her face all red. She beckons to me to come and I gather up my skirts in my hands and run to meet her.

"Well, my dear, if you knew the goings on! While I had gone downstairs to take some compositions to the small girls' classes, a girl, Marguerite van Helz, you know, the dark-haired girl who is so grown up for her age, a real Flemish girl... briefly... Marguerite found some means to annoy the Fräulein, the German mistress of the children, in a way that will not bring her much luck.

"Here is the story: Marguerite had been punished and as punishment had been condemned to do the washing under the supervision of old Katherine, an odious scullion.

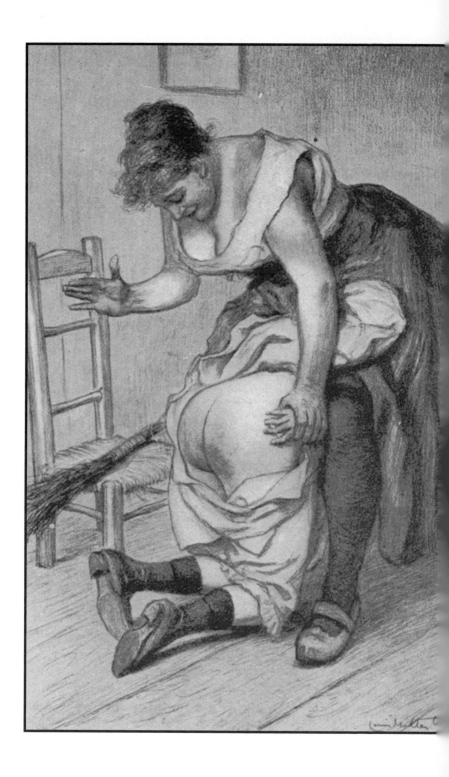

Haven't you seen her yet? No!—I do not wish you to fall into her dirty paws, it appears that this shrew takes horrible pleasure in humiliating young girls who come under her power. It's the revenge, you see, of people of low extraction who do not forgive us for being rich and refined, and happy afterwards, for my dear little puss, we shall not always remain in this foul place. I am straying from the story—so Marguerite, dressed after the fashion of a washer-woman, directed her steps towards the scullery which is public, as the President gives the people of the village the right to wash their linen once a week.

"It is already sufficiently humiliating for a girl of high-birth to undergo the promiscuity of those chubby-cheeked and gossipy shrews, but it is nothing compared to what old Katherine had imagined for the victim that the President had put under her sway... that is to say under the beetle... you see?"

"I confess, I replied, that I shall do all I can not to undergo that punishment; I still prefer the ruler on the hands than to be exposed to the coarse language and scurrilities of those vile women!"

"That is to be seen, answered Georgette, smilingly, one can see that you have not yet been punished. When it will happen, and my poor little kitten, it is inevitable in a "dump" like this, you will perhaps change your mind... One cannot escape a whipping... it is written and there is nothing that can prevent the debasing ceremony of the turning up of your skirt!"

"Don't let us speak of it Georgette, you cannot imagine the effect that that word produces on my nerves... I shall have a fit!"

"Oh! what a nervous little puss!" Hence old Katherine, under the false pretence that Marguerite van Helz did her work badly found nothing better to do than to force her bodily over a tub and to lift up her skirts in order to beat her with the wet beetle which she brandished like a fury.

Screams, howls, protestations—"It's ignoble, let me go, *etc., etc.*"—You know the words and the music that usually accompany these sort of ceremonies.

The women laughed and giggled, delighted at this unexpected bit of good luck which allowed them to witness the quaint spectacle of a rich young girl whipped on her bottom. The drawers of Marguerite were an obstacle which old Katherine, in spite of all her strength, could not overcome, taken up as she was in holding her prey in the requisite posture. It was one of the other of the women who gave the help needed,

and who undid the drawers that fell about the poor girl's ankles. When the bottom spread out its nudity before the eyes of the audience that formed the circle, the laughs and the quibbles that followed, aggravated the distraught state that poor Marguerite was in, who pressed her knees one against the other with all the strength she possessed.

It is Lucie, the maid, who told me what had happened; she was present and she said that she had never seen such an ignoble sight. The peasant women interpolated Marguerite... "Oh my dear, with such cushions on your seat, you don't hurt yourself when you fall..."

"But yes," said another, "she must have broken her watch glass. It is cracked along the middle. It brings luck to own a medal like that one," chaffed another, and the guffaws and the sarcasm lashed the poor girl—they are really vile people—you can imagine the rest, old Katherine raised her beetle and administered a terrible spanking to Marguerite, whom Fräulein, who had been a witness of this barbarous scene, held in her bent posture. Lucie told me that Marguerite received at least twenty blows with the beetle; her bottom was all red; it is not a terrible punishment, but in this case the shame of being chastised publicly outweighed the pain. I am positive that Marguerite would have preferred a worse flagellation at the hands of the President rather than have been obliged to show her bottom in front of all these women.

"But this is all an awful dream," I murmured, running my hands over my eyes.

And in fact I could not believe such a thing. The scandalous whipping that Marguerite van Helz had had did not present itself to me as a reality. My decorous being, my upbringing of a good young girl... all my tenderness revolted against the treatment which brought down a woman to the same level of a dog, mercilessly whipped... even thus, an animal is not affected except by physical suffering, while a modest young girl... good God... Why must it be that the most indelicate parts of the human body should be chosen as the traditional site for inflicting the whip... The news of a chastisement on the shoulders would have found me submissive, or at least resigned to my fate, since coercive chastisement is a usual thing in a reformatory—but the whipping ! In writing these lines I blush to the roots of my hair and yet I was to acquire a few days after, for three consecutive years, the sad habit of lifting my skirt in the classroom and in public.

Georgette, indignant, continued the recital of this experience which unfortunately was daily repeated in this reformatory, whose disciplinary programme and school régimen seemed to be directed to the bottom of their students rather than to their brains!

"Yes, my dear, Marguerite without even pulling up her drawers, as soon as she was on her feet, in a movement of anger, slapped the Dean who had been smiling stupidly while contemplating the reddened face of her, whom she had been holding."—And then?

"Then, my dear little one, I frankly declare that I would not like to be in Marguerite's shoes... Fräulein made a report with this and that... You can imagine if she envenomed the facts... the fact remains that Marguerite is locked-up since an hour. When the President will read this week's marks she will enlighten us as to the fate of the little Flemish girl... You can be sure that you will witness something like a whipping... brrr! I am shivering merely at the thought of it... Good-bye my little puss, I must run away as I have a lesson to learn, and I have not the slightest desire of showing you my bottom..."

She kissed me, offering her pretty little mouth in a
pretty pout, of charming roguishness, and then escaped in the
direction of the study rooms, leaving me all abashed.

"Well, Mademoiselle Lucette, what are you doing
there, staring about vacantly; recess is over, hurry up and get
your books... I believe that the time for severely dealing with
you is not far!"

I stared, it was Miss Elisa; without waiting for more, I
ran to the classroom.

I was just in time, the bell of the little Gothic chapel
rained its crystal pearls in the pure air of this happy country—and
yet this book is not dedicated to bucolics nor to eclogues; yet in
spite of the daily wretchedness there are minutes of happiness
when it is good to be alive.

Two by two the boarders belonging to the big classes go
to the classroom, where one can already hear the hubbub of the
day-students, who in the absence of the teacher twittered
joyously like little birds in an aviary.

Our arrival and especially that of Miss Elisa, who
precedes us, creates order as by enchantment. It is the history
class. Miss Elisa talks to us of the Affair of the Necklace,
deplorably insisting on the public flagellation of the Comtesse
de la Mothe. I am thinking that she is not the only one, and I am
more interested in the fate of little Margot than that of that lady,
whom Miss Elisa seems to enjoy so much in detailing her
scandalous life.

Suddenly, as I was musing, haunted by this continual
fear, the door opened wide and Madame de Quirinodo, followed
by Fräulein and by Madame Schweinpelz, the housekeeper,
made a royal entrance, full of dignity and of elegance.

We all got up, boarders as well as day-students, as a
mark of respectful deference. With a loose gesture of a beautiful
hand, she told us to sit down, and after a few pleasant words to
our teacher she began to read the marks of the week. She began
with the day-students; for them, bad marks had as a sole
consequence extra tasks and a warning to their parents; who
could whip their daughters if that was their custom... For us,

boarders, the punishments meant a spanking, a whipping with a rod, a whipping with switches, all depending on the extent of the short-coming... The announcement of the punishment was made aloud, and one died of shame on hearing the repressed chuckles of the day-students, who, if they were not exempted from a whipping from their parents, did not undergo any publicity in their punishment.

When each one knew the fate which was reserved to her, Madame de Quirinodo lifted her lovely head, haughtily and pretentiously, and her hands resting on Miss Elisa's desk, she spoke of that "thing" which we boarders never ceased to think of.

"Young ladies, one of you, one who needs to watch the deviations of her conduct, has permitted herself to rebel in an unheard of manner against one of her teachers. I shall not give any details, let it suffice that tomorrow afternoon, Mademoiselle Marguerite van Helz, whose parents have given me in writing entire latitude as regards physical punishments, shall be whipped naked in the gymnasium in the presence of boarders and day-students of all the three classes—that is to say the young girls, the intermediate and the big girls—I hope that this punishment, which shall be severe, will be for you food for meditation and a salutary example; it is to the boarders that I am speaking to!"

Then, after having spoken with Miss Elisa in a low voice, who hypocritically nodded with her head, she left the classroom with a royal gait, in a swishing of her elegant silk underclothing.

I remember a poem of Oscar Wilde: *The Ballad of Reading Gaol*, when the condemned prisoner waits for dawn when he must die, the other prisoners think of him, who no more will see the sunshine, and their prayers ascend from all the cells in a transport of touching pity.

Certainly, our little playmate was not going to die the following day, but none of us could sleep that night, that preceded the day when all naked, without a veil to protect her pudicity, Marguerite was whipped in the presence of a hundred young girls, in front of her teachers, in front of the maids and, what I was to learn later, in front of a man—what a shame!

I was feverish, and when the bell rang, when Miss Elisa came to open the doors of our rooms, I was broken down with fatigue, and in an anxious and nervous state, irritable to the point of breaking into tears over nothing.

In the yard, during morning recess, naturally we spoke but of that, and it was impatiently that I awaited the hour when the sentence was to be executed.

Even if this is not to my credit, candour obliges me to say in these memoirs, that this feeling increased as the hands of the clock approached the hour of the ceremony.

This perversity, which impels the mob around the steps of the guillotine, had mastered the excessive irritability of our nerves. Such sights were to complete the disorder of our poor little wills of young women.

At two o'clock the day-students in front and we others followed the crowd, went to the small gymnasium where a professor from Brussels came every week to give us lessons in physics as well as in chemistry.

A queer little man, formerly a priest, intelligent, yet sorry-looking—engrossed to the point of madness in occultism—and most monstrously perverted.

It was, besides, he who was the cause of events which I shall describe later.

We seated ourselves according to our respective ranks, the small girls, following a new command, were not to witness the punishment, and there were only girls between thirteen- and eighteen-years of age.

Against the blackboard, a small ladder had been placed; it was the instrument of torture around which seven or eight strong maidservants, Flemish women, submissive and mean, served as escort to her, who had the official rôle of whipper, that is to say, old Katherine.

"I pity Marguerite," whispered Georgette, who was my neighbour.

There was a great hubbub in the corridor; the door opened, and Madame de Quirinodo walked in, followed by the victim, who was surrounded by Fräulein, the housekeeper and the teachers of the different classes. Miss Elisa stood near us, switch hanging from her waist, with the object of establishing order amongst the audience in case any troublesome commotion were to be manifested during the punishment.

When the culprit made her appearance, all eyes stared at her. At the sight of all these faces, that reflected thoughts most incongruous and most contradictory Marguerite van Helz began to cry.

"Oh, Madame, Madame, please don't—not here—I beg you? I beseech you, not in front of everybody."

The President did not reply, but went to make sure that the switches had been soaked in water and that they were pliant and cutting.

Satisfied with her inspection, she approached Marguerite, who was sobbing with a big grief of a small child, which made her so sweet that I would have done I know not what, to have been able to take her in my arms and to caress her gently—very gently.

Madame de Quirinodo, cold and feline as a panther, whose powerful and supple grace she possessed, was not moved by the beautiful and lovely eyes steeped in tears.

"Mademoiselle van Helz, since your parents have given me the right to act with you and for your good as I think best, I warn you that you shall be whipped naked in front of all these young ladies, and I hope that it will be the sole punishment of this sort that you will receive during your sojourn here!"

The poor girl on hearing these words fell to her knees, with hands joined together, she supplicated, stammering incoherent words, "pardons and pardons," intersected by sobs.

We others on our benches were all blushing with shame and indignation on seeing a young girl of our class, of our age, humiliating herself to such a degree.

The affront reflected on me, on Georgette, on Suzanne d'Alleuse, on everyone—but fear prevented us from protesting—and the interest of this spectacle had excited our unhealthy curiosity to such a degree, that we all would have pointed our thumbs downwards, as used to do the vestals who refused mercy to the gladiator in the sports of the arena.

It was Fräulein who took on herself to undress Marguerite, while two servants lifted up her arms and legs in order to oblige her to have her shoes undone, and her bodice unbuttoned.

A young bosom, round shoulders, and the milky whiteness of her neck, a bust of only a young girl, this was what was at first seen of Marguerite's velvety skin.

Then her skirts fell down and beneath the skirts amongst the delicate tints of her silken underwear one could see the arch silhouette of a young girl in stays and in drawers.

Margot had her back turned to us, and I could not repress an amused smile at a frolicsome little detail—it was a little end of a chemise which showed through a narrow slit of her drawers decked with lace—a slit very, very narrow, just large enough to quickly allow the satisfaction of a pressing little need.

Her corset, quickly untied, showed a bosom well-developed, and the roundness of her globes, whose little tips indiscreetly stood out, beneath the fine cambric of her chemise lined with mauve ribbons.

And this undressing took place with a cinematographic rapidity, the last garments, drawers, stockings and chemise, were quickly untied, taken off and put on a chair.

A gentle murmur, quickly repressed by a severe look from Madame de Quirinodo, greeted the nudity of Marguerite.

This murmur was entirely one of admiration. Figure to yourself a lovely little doll in flesh, prettily rounded bosom, and behind at the right place; a contour of hips to make a sculptor in love with the elegance of classic beauty go crazy, thighs slender and tapering, knees with dimples and tiny pink feet, exquisite to devour.

Imagine all that, a dainty head of a young girl in tears; lovely little face with sweet eyes drowned in tears; lovely little face, crowned by ebony hair whose fringes coiled themselves on the nape of her neck, held by a big knot of red velvet.

Figure to yourself, there when one cannot look without violent emotion—but there are things one cannot write of; and in spite of everything you shall have an imperfect description of our little friend Margot, such as she appeared to us before being whipped on the ignominious ladder.

This absolutely true scene that I witnessed carried me to the worst epochs of the middle-ages. I lived over again the infernal hours of the Inquisition, and it was the nudity of this young girl, white and pure as a lily amongst the sombre dresses of the teachers and the servants that made me invoke the customs that I should have believed henceforth abolished.

Marguerite was tied to the steps of the ladder in such a manner that the arms stretched upwards forced the muscles of the poor little girl to stretch painfully, and her legs slightly parted were immobilised from beneath. The victim, her face turned towards the rungs of the ladder, offered us the delightful spectacle of a delicate neck, and the slim waist that showed off in a provoking manner the roundness of her bottom.

I told you the impression that I had the first time that I saw that part of the female anatomy. My friends and myself could not take our eyes from the lovely round cheeks separated by a deep groove as far as the shadowy mystery of her thighs.

Already old Katherine had chosen one of the rods, a bundle of birch canes tied together by a silk ribbon.

Spiteful and cross-grained, wishing to wreak vengeance on the skin of this aristocratic bottom, she tried the instrument on the palms of her hands while Madame de Quirinodo and the authorities seated themselves in order to comfortably enjoy the picture.

When the switch whistled in the silence, my shoulders stiffened, my eyes shut, and in spite of myself I convulsively pressed together that part of my body on which I sat, and which was serving as a target, in the case of Marguerite, to the tormenting fury of the switches.

A scream, the first one, pierced my ears like a gimlet—on the white flesh of the immaculate bottom a red streak was outlined, scarring transversely the whole of the female cheeks.

The second, the third lash fell with despairing regularity and as a dozen strokes had already been applied in the midst of the sobs and the howls of Marguerite, we saw that the bottom had become red and shiny, of a red colour which made this part of the body still more indecent, and specially naked, due to this burning redness that showed off in striking relief, next to the ivory whiteness of the small of the back and of the thighs.

"Mercy—ooh!—Good God! Oooh! you are hurting me—oooh! I am suffering—Par—don—" One should hear these words coming from the sweet mouth of a young girl to know all the humiliation of a whipping.

We were all as pale as death, instinctively I was squeezing myself against Georgette and the warmth of her body penetrating mine at the hips and thighs plunged me into a most undefineable and most equivocal sensation.

The convulsive movements of Margot's bottom answered each bite of the switch and the poor girl absolutely distracted by the pain staggered on her knees, loosening little by little the pressure of her thighs one against the other.

"Oh!—look—there!"

I followed the direction of Georgette's finger timidly.

I become as red as a peony. "Oh, yes, it is like a pretty shell, so pink, so delicate!" And in replying to my friend I dared not look at her for I felt her heart beating faster, and the warm breath of her exquisitely made mouth brushed my cheeks. I was swooning in a sweet languor.

The tormenting rhythm of the switches, whipping the naked flesh revived my terror. It was too much! How could one thus whip flesh so tender, so dimpled, so sweet. Twenty times at least I was on the point of crying out: "Mercy, do not whip her any more—have mercy!" But prudence prevented me from committing a blunder, the result of which would have been, that I would have been tied to the ladder without saving Margot from the rest of the outrageous whipping which she had to receive to the finish.

As a pitiless blow descended on the small bottom at the summit of the right cheek, a ruby formed like a bead, then slowly glided down the inflamed skin making a dark red line—it was blood.

I thought I was going to faint. Marguerite's screams redoubled, and a curious thing, the poor girl who just a minute ago had been humbly supplicating, terrorised by the whip, now screamed her disgust, shouted out insults, cursing her torturers.

"Aaa!—it's—ooh! vi—ile ! Enough… aaah! pigs! pigs!—I'll—oh; kill you all!"

A burst of saucy laughter and impertinent laughter was Madame de Quirinodo's only reply.

Nevertheless, the President made a sign to the whipper to add a little more vigour to her blows. The blood spotted the ivory flesh and two thin threads of purple ran down her thighs dropping on to the floor where a small dark stain became bigger and bigger.

"Ah—God, God! Mercy! Mercy!" The poor girl turned her head around; stiffened and then her eyes turned up, and her head fell slackly on her shoulder.

"Stop!" Madame de Quirinodo simply said to the servant. "She has fainted—besides she has had her share—give her smelling salts and carry her to the sick ward."

We came out of this hell, besotted, incapable of collecting our thoughts together. As we were whispering in small groups, the teachers intervened.

"Go and play—do not stay here—if you do not obey do not forget that there is always a place on your bottoms to receive a good whipping!"

Thus recalled to the reality of our sad existence, we went towards the tennis lawn—could we do otherwise than obey? Poor Margot's torture did not stop there.

We heard through the indiscretion of the servant of the ward that Margot had again been punished the next day because she had refused to show her bruised bottom to a lady superintendent who wanted to find out the efficacy of corporal punishments.

For a long time I wondered what this lady, a Russian countess, staying in the country at K—— could have to do in this affair. Now that I know life, I do not doubt that the poor creature came to find in the whipped bottom sensations which she was feverishly searching for.

For this reason, in front of this countess, Margot underwent another ordeal.

She was made to lie down naked on her hospital bed and while two servants immobilised her, her breasts tendered, the President, armed with a strong elastic, lashed the pink tips of the young breasts.

Placing one extremity of the elastic on the pink bud of her breasts, she drew the elastic and then let it go, it bit the delicate flesh, and made the poor little girl jump into the arms of her, who was making her undergo this atrocious punishment.

Poor Margot, in writing these lines, I again see the harmonious curves of your lovely body—at that time you were one of the tender Bilitis of the reformatory—did you not reveal to me that beneath the thorns of life—the roses blossomed, lovely and troubling? A tear forms, moved as I am even now, at the tip of my lashes.

After the severe punishment that Marguerite van Helz had received in front of all the students of the boarding-house, for several days I was kept in awe by what I had seen, and the same was true of all my terrorised playmates who showed good behaviour, more than exemplary.

But that which must happen always happens; nothing can prevent the fatality of certain things that are due, and that one which was to rob my bottom of its school virginity happened quite naturally, since the efforts of the teachers and of the playmates only tended towards forcing me to undress and to show this interesting part of my anatomy.

In the reformatory, which Madame de Quirinodo governed, informing and telling tales was cultivated to the point of becoming a match to civil institution.

A playmate, I do not know which one, for I would have

scratched her with pleasure, went and told Miss Elisa that I had spent all my morning study time in drawing caricatures showing her in postures not flattering to her self-respect.

Miss Elisa immediately concluded with just cause that I had not had time to learn my lessons, and without hesitating she questioned me first on my geography lesson which had been prepared for that day.

I did not know my lesson and I had hoped that having been questioned all the week, in all the other lessons, and having received the very best marks, that I would be left in peace that day. But it was not to be thus, and no sooner had we seated ourselves than Miss Elisa turned towards me and called my name.

"Mademoiselle Lucette."

I was so little expecting this that I felt myself become quite pale suddenly.

The authority of our teachers was such that the least remark, the least warning was enough to completely distract us.

I shall always remember the question which she asked me. It was the bed of the Danube that I had to draw on the blackboard indicating the position of the cities which it flowed through.

More dead than alive, obnubilated by the consciousness that I did not know the least thing about this question, I went to the blackboard.

The whole thing was lamentable. With difficulty I stammered some confused explanations, disconcerted by the ironic look of my teacher, while I floundered with visible embarrassment.

At each of my replies, the giggling of the pupils made me forget everything and it was with nameless anguish that I heard Miss Elisa conclude thus:

"Madamoiselle Lucette, you do not know a word of your lesson, would have done far better to have opened your book than to have made disgusting caricatures. In short, I think it is high time to be less indulgent towards you; you are, besides, sufficiently well informed as regards the practices of this school, to be able to bear like your playmates the punishments which it is customary to inflict on those who are lazy and undisciplined—you

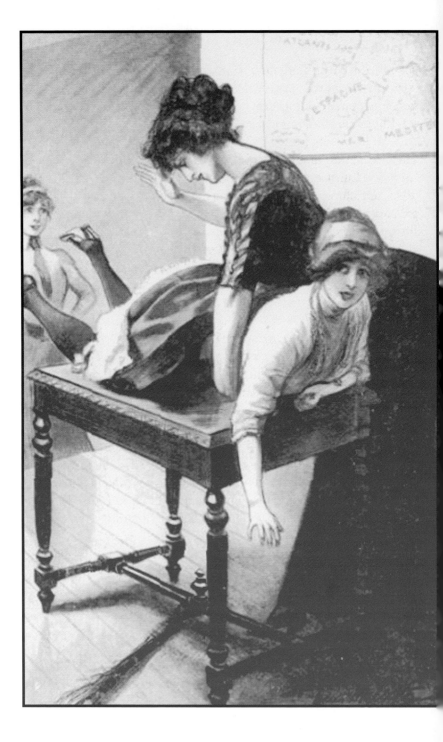

shall be whipped; come up here near my desk."

Then all at once I became a coward. I was so afraid of being whipped that I threw myself at my teacher's feet and joining my hands I beseeched her to forgive me.

"For this time," I said, "let me be Miss, I promise that I shall never do it again, forgive me I beseech you!"

"Lucette, I have already forgiven you at least ten times; your punishment is merited and as I hate all this useless grimacing, I shall ask you to turn your back to your comrades, lift up your skirts, to let fall your drawers and to show these young ladies your big naked bottom, that they may see the sound whipping that you will get. For the first time I shall be satisfied with spanking your bottom with my hands—hurry up! Be quick."

Tears darkened my vision and prevented me from seeing, my ears buzzed and I could not hear, and the sobs in my throat prevented me from speaking.

A slap fell on my cheek before I could make the slightest movement to hinder it.

"*Oh la, la!*"

"Will you hurry up and obey me, will you?"

"Yes—yes, Mi—iss!"

I kept as motionless as a doormouse. Miss Elisa slapped me two or three times making my cheeks turn vermilion coloured.

She had taken hold of my hair which was dressed in a big chignon on my nape and she was violently shaking me, while railing at me in a hoarse voice.

"Will you obey—will you lift up your dresses—drop your drawers—tender your bottom! Ah, Mademoiselle is ashamed, Mademoiselle does not wish to show us her moon. Mademoiselle does not wish to appear ridiculous—in that case, Mademoiselle had but to study her lesson!"

All these vehement apostrophes were intersected by slaps. The pain that Miss Elisa was causing me in pulling my hair made me yell like a dog being beaten. I no longer knew what I was doing.

"Yes Miss, I am obeying. There, do not beat me any

more. You see, I am obeying. *Oh la la!* Oh, my head!"

In fact I was obeying in haste, but awkwardly.

I lifted up my skirts with my two hands, showing my stockings and my bottom imprisoned in drawers. Arrived at this point of the indecent undressing exacted of me, Miss Elisa seeing that I hesitated to unbutton my drawers railed at me once again.

"Open the slit of your drawers and bend down to show your behind!"

"Oh, Miss!"

"Well?"

"My drawers are closed ones!"

"Silly, lower them and bend over this table."

I undid the ribbon and felt very upset; all my pudicity, all my refinement of a young virgin shattered by the horrible affront I was about to receive. I felt the frail garment slip down my legs and twist itself around my ankles. "Bend down and lift up your chemise!"

"Oh, Miss. You do it. I cannot. It is too shameful!"

"I desire that you yourself expose your bottom. Go on, bend down!

I obeyed and I lay over the table leaning on my stomach, the points of my feet just touching the floor, in a posture tendering my bottom in a shamefully provoking manner.

"Lift up your chemise!"

Miss Elisa is standing up next to me, my hands grip the frail garment which veils my posterior charms, and I raise the curtain. The cold air tickles my naked flesh. The cup is drunk to the dregs. I show everything. I, Lucette de Hêtraie, my naked bottom to my playmates, amongst whom I hear a few laugh.

Miss Elisa did not hurry to spank me, she enjoyed the beautiful sight that I was granting. I say beautiful sight without false modesty, for at that time I already knew that I was beautiful physically, as I had admired myself from all angles in front of my looking-glass, privy to my coquettishness.

After having scrutinised the ivory roundness which it was her mission to turn into red, Miss Elisa encircled my slim waist with her right arm, spread my chemise and my skirt as high as she could over my shoulders and the dance began. She beat me in a painful and ridiculous manner, as they beat very little girls, with her hand. And yet I assure you the pain was as burning as could be; after the first slap I pressed the cheeks of my bottom together as tightly as I could to diminish the surface tendered, and to avoid the play of the thighs which would have shown the audience more than it was necessary to show.

Flac! Flac! Flac! The characteristic noise of a naked bottom that is being slapped, rang in my ears and made me cry out "*Oh, la la!*" each time that the stiff and heavy hand of my teacher came violently into contact with the satin skin.

I felt the burn in my fleshy parts, that I spread out in all its roundness, in spite of myself. The frantic dance that my bottom executed at each slap must have been a most amusing sight if I was to judge by the choking laughter of my playmates.

The pain of the punishment was not sufficiently violent to prevent my hearing the whispering amongst the students; their little laughs exasperated me; in spite of the pain that I felt I would have wished that Miss Elisa would beat them all to punish them. Oh, how happy I would have been to see the bottoms palpitate and jump beneath the blows of a whip.

Now, the sensation of burning that had seemed at the beginning quite tolerable so that I had not been able to help thinking "So this is all!" became frightful and the screams that I had held back till then escaped me, although I did all I could to bravely bear this beating, which was to initiate my seat to the delights of flagellation.

My supplications did not differ much from those of my playmates when they were in similar postures.

We were all like little girls, and the only words that we could utter were exclamations of pain or cries of supplication.

My bottom for this beating, which was the first but not the last time in my life, was slapped some forty times.

My flesh was so painful that when I was sent back to my seat I felt that I was sitting on a red-hot iron, inasmuch as Miss Elisa had not allowed me to put on my drawers—I had been obliged, skirts lowered, to take my seat, my ankles enclosed in my drawers whose fine linen trailed lamentably in the dust.

Once seated I dared not raise my eyes as I felt the looks of all my playmates fixed on me.

Suzanne Lance, who is my right-hand neighbour, maliciously pushed me with her elbow.

"What, it's warm down below!"

I blushed but did not reply, only a tear formed on my lashes.

Georgette, who was my left-hand neighbour, comforted me in a low voice, while the teacher corrected a student's copy book.

"My poor little thing, you are suffering. Tonight I have something with which to open your door. I shall come and comfort you; to nurse you. Yes?"

The bell rang for recess.

Humbly I turned to Miss Elisa:

"May I put on my drawers now, Miss ?"

"Yes, you can do so, you have been punished sufficiently for this time."

The pain of my bottom is less, and I do justice to the tea and to the bread and butter which we get at tea-time.

Then that night I infringed on the rules of the school. Georgette found means of opening the door of my room although Miss Elisa had locked it.

Georgette! Georgette! In writing these lines, I think of you who were so kind, and although the threat of the whip is no longer here to affect me, I still blush at the remembrance of certain things.

III

A BOOK ON reformatories is sufficiently given up to monotonous descriptions of one beating following another, and as nothing resembles one flagellation as much as another, I should not risk boring my readers were it not that Madame de Quirinodo's and Miss Elisa's imagination brought new diversions into the chastisements which we had to undergo.

This woman, impelled by a sadism more frequent than one would believe in a woman, was perfectly acquainted with the psychology of flagellation.

She was a passionate flagellant; she loved to whip young girls... our pain gave her pleasure... roused her sensuality like the shame which she knew how to inflict, and does, with diabolic knowledge.

Shame! Can one imagine that there exist on earth beings, women, beautiful and educated women, for vice does not always accompany ugliness and ignorance, who take pleasure in humiliating young girls, giving them up to innumerable affronts.

Enough books have already been written on flagellation making it unnecessary to further study this perversion. I am, besides, not qualified to do this, being content in these few notes to record the scenes that I lived through, and the impressions that I felt.

To be truthful, I must frankly confess that I liked to be whipped by Miss Elisa, and even more by Madame de Quirinodo.

With her, all the details of the torture were for me, an inexhaustible source of cerebral and physical pleasures.

I liked to be at her feet, to make her a sort of sacrifice of all my pride, the gift of all my being, in humbly tendering towards her the roundness of my flesh which was to docilely lend itself to the vigour of her arm.

When Madame de Quirinodo was a witness of the whippings, I was in a mental state, in a way, comparable to the aberrations of certain fanatics.

To know that the beautiful eyes of the President were fixed on me, there where my flesh ought not to be revealed, plunged me in the most delicious sensations, and while she beat me with a violence which always made me scream, I in no degree moderated the immodest dance of my buttocks, knowing like that great lady of whom Brantome speaks, that the "twisting of my body" gave her pleasure.

Nevertheless, besides the pleasure which she experienced in seeing the beautiful adolescent bodies writhe beneath the rods, the President loved, beyond all else, to move the pudicity of the virgins and to colour their pink cheeks with a bright red of shame.

She never missed an opportunity to humiliate us, and it was she who had invented the idea of whipping us with naked bottoms in front of the day-students, who thus maintained towards us a crushing superiority, that of not having shown us their bottoms.

This feeling was so genuine that we all preferred being whipped till the blood came in front of the other boarders, rather than be beaten with a hand in front of these little hussies from the city, who did not in any way abstain from mocking us when ever an opportunity presented itself.

We were in their eyes in a state of humiliating slavery, and we all sought the opportunity to wreak vengeance on the minxes.

We had, once only, the divine pleasure of avenging ourselves on the bottom of one of these modest and insolent young ladies, of all the ill-treatments which our poor bottoms had endured in their presence.

It was during a walk along the seashore, in the sand dunes, that the thing occurred.

It was simple and brief.

Miss Elisa, who conducted the walk, had strayed into a copse with about ten girls, collecting flowers.

Seven or eight young girls of the big class to which I belong had rested themselves, seated on the grass, waiting for the return of Miss Elisa.

We were chattering pleasantly... when on the top of a small mound, the silhouette of a young girl of fifteen-years-old was outlined, Minnie W, daughter of a rich London Merchant, who followed Madame Quirinodo's classes, but as a day-student.

We had already noticed how very slanderous and haughty this young and very pretty girl was. She was of those who did not spare either sarcasm or jeers when fate caused one of us to be whipped in her presence.

This young girl did wrong in looking at us insolently and in greeting us in a slightly too patronising manner, in our opinion.

How the idea to punish her instantaneously developed in our brains, I cannot say; at any rate, after looking at each other we rushed upon her.

She was coming back from golf and still held a stick in her hand. She tried to defend herself, but in a second she was held by the wrists, while one of us thrust her handkerchief into her mouth to prevent her screaming.

She was then at our mercy. Georgette bent her down, forcing her to tender her bottom, while I lifted up her skirts.

She had open drawers, and we opened the slits as wide as we could, and lifting her chemise over her back, we could contemplate at our ease a big and lovely bottom, of one who had never been whipped.

Marguerite during this time had picked up a rod of furze.

She took it upon herself to apply the whipping, and did it conscientiously, whipping the chubby big bottom as hard as she could.

The beautiful girl was far from thinking this operation a pleasant one, for she kicked and struggled so much, that we had to join all our forces to hold her, until she took her share of a sound flogging.

When we lowered the skirts, she had received some twenty blows with a rod, with the result that her bottom had taken the colour of a ripe tomato.

She did not thank us, nor ask for more. Without turning her head she ran away as fast as she could, fearing to see anyone and to be obliged to relate the humiliating punishment which she had just undergone.

This little incident had made us all gay, and when Miss Elisa came back with the others shortly after the scene that I have just described, she found us all smiling, and our faces beaming with satisfaction.

Miss Elisa never found out anything and, the persons chiefly concerned in this matter never saying a word about it, there were no consequences.

Otherwise, I shiver as I think of it, there would never have been enough switches in the Reformatory to beat our poor bottoms.

This little incident was for us a real treat, for if we sometimes liked to be whipped, it was not disagreeable to do it to others.

Between us we would whip each other often enough for the sole pleasure of showing our bottoms and of slapping the appetising moons... There often followed certain liberties, and "little innocent games" which decency does not allow me to relate.

But, I am digressing from the principal subject matter of this chapter, which was to explain this strange desire which the President had of humiliating us by all sorts of means, of her invention.

And she would find queer and frightful ones. I leave you to judge from the following small anecdote, the blushing and abashed heroine of which I was.

It was in September, and the cold weather made itself felt, especially in the morning as the dormitories were not yet heated, as they were repairing the radiators which distributed a sweet warmth in the building.

The desire to be lazy and to stay in bed longer made me curl up in my sheets, while at the same time, waiting in an exquisite anguish, the hour of getting up, which was at half-past seven.

"My word," I thought to myself, "it is so good in bed that I shall simply tell Miss Elisa that I am ill... they can't eat me up."

Delighted by my idea, I waited for the hour of getting up, and when Miss Elisa came to open my door, she found me in bed with the languishing mien of a sick person.

"Well Lucette, will you not get up?"

"Miss, I do not feel very well, I feel tired... with a little headache!"

"Very well, stay in bed. I shall tell the President who will notify the doctor."

Half-an-hour later, the President came to see me, questioned me, made me put out my tongue, and left, looking at me with an ironic smile, which left me musing, in spite of the goody-goody feeling that I was enjoying in staying in bed. The morning went by without anything happening. Towards two o'clock in the afternoon, the doctor came to see me. He was a small old man, spiteful and sneaking. He made me put out my tongue and felt my pulse, examined me patiently and left, telling the President that there was nothing the matter, just a bit of constipation, and that he would write out a prescription.

In saying this he looked at Madame de Quirinodo and Miss Elisa who answered him with a smile.

I began to be anxious, without understanding, nevertheless, the trick they were to play on me.

Then these ladies left, leaving me alone for an hour.

I began to be bored all by myself in my room, when the sound of many feet in the corridor made me involuntarily quake. They were coming!

The door of my room opened and there entered Madame de Quirinodo, Miss Elisa, Fräulein and Miss Schweinpelz, the housekeeper; the latter carried under her arm, hidden by a cloth, an object whose utility I could not immediately make out.

My doubts did not last long, for the housekeeper, having placed the towel on the table, came near my bed carefully carrying, guess what?... An irrigator!

"My child, the doctor has ordered that you should take an enema every day; we have prepared a decoction of mallow, hurry up and take this small clyster, and do not let it get cold."

I was dumbfounded. To take an enema is always a

ridiculous ceremony, a grotesque medicament, due to the way it is administered.

I looked at the four mocking women without replying. For sure I would have raised no objection to take the clyster by myself, but in front of all these persons, no! no!

"Go on, Lucette, hurry up, we are waiting, come to the edge of the bed and turn what you know this way, Miss Schweinpelz will do the rest, she is used to these little operations."

"But Madam... in front of all of you... oh ! Leave me the thing... I will take it by myself..."

"You are stupid, if you will not do as you are bidden, you will be whipped, and then these ladies will hold you while Miss Schweinpelz will apply the instrument."

There was nothing to be done. Dying with shame, I turned my face towards the wall and offered my buttocks to the group, and to my apothecary in skirts.

A hand took off the sheets, another lifted up my chemise, revealing the round nudity of my fleshy parts.

Then on my skin, I felt indiscreet fingers which opened the plump cheeks of my seat... and the operation went on without any obstacle, under the curious gaze of the four spectators.

When I had absorbed the contents of the apparatus, my chemise was modestly lowered as the curtain is lowered when a ɪy is finished.

The four teachers left, leaving me alone with my shame and the remembrance of this stupid scene of which I was the grotesque victim.

I give you my word, that if that enema cured me of a sickness that had not existed, it also cured me of the desire to be lazy.

All the more so as this humiliating ceremony was repeated ays, although the day following I manifested the desire to go to class, thinking thus to stop this Molierish comedy.

But it was going from Charybide to Scylla... and besides that, I received a whipping in class.

This is how it happened:

At three o'clock during the German class, taught by Fräulein, a servant opened the door, and having greeted the teacher she asked for permission to speak to me.

With the latter's consent, the servant cried out in the middle of the silence:

"Mademoiselle de Hêtraie, the President lets you know you are immediately to go to the sick-ward to take your enema."

A Homeric burst of laughter was the consequence of this order, the teacher herself was laughing.

Blushing with indignation, with shame and anger, I began to stamp my foot, and crazy with anger to have thus been ridiculed in front of all my playmates, I replied coarsely I know not what.

Then Fräulein established silence, and, followed by the servant, she came towards me, took me by the ear and led me to the desk. With the aid of the maid, for was struggling like a devil, she bent me dow tucked up my clothes and unbuttoned my drawers in a twinkle of an eye.

A rod hung beneath her desk, she took hold of it and began to whip me with such a force that I did not wait long before begging for mercy, supplicating that they spare me, and that I would do whatever they wished.

She let me get up, and my eyes red with crying, my ears purple with shame, I followed the servant to the sick-ward.

Life continued monotonously apart from the punishments which we all underwent, for one reason or another.

A year went by, there were no vacations for us boarders, but for the day-students it was the time of the year when they went to the fashionable sea shore resorts.

Discipline slightly relaxed in the boarding house of Mme. de Quirinodo, and apart from some laughable little whippings, we reached, without having suffered much, the new semester.

This time we had the pleasure of initiating a new girl to the disciplinary régimen of the school.

She came on an October afternoon in a superb car, with a chauffeur and a footman.

Through thes panes of the study, we saw her get out of her car, beautiful as a queen whose gait she possessed, magnificent in her haughty beauty, at least such as it is concerned to imagine a queen.

We already knew, through talk amongst the maids, the name of the young and beautiful girl, and we also knew the reasons that brought her to this reformatory.

Kate MacAnnay was a lovely girl, nineteen-years-old, whose father was one of the richest land owners in Scotland.

A thwarted love affair had brought the proud young girl into the claws of Mme. de Quirinodo.

She loved a penniless young officer, and as usual the paternal will had shattered this tender love.

As a pretext that the beautiful girl had flirted overmuch with her lover, her father one day obliged her to cross the Channel. She landed at Zeebrugge, from whence she was driven to the boarding house where they were to subdue her will, which rebelled against all constraint.

The father had given strict orders to the President that no punishment be spared with his daughter.

"You must break her indomitable nature," he had written to Mme. de Quirinodo, "and therefore I give you free scope." And Kate MacAnnay arrived one lovely October day and we were all struck by her beauty.

She was, however, sympathetic only on condition that we admired her through the eyes of an artist, admired the loveliness of her face and the exquisite proportions of her body, for as regards the rest, the haughty expression and the pretentious pride which she manifested when we were introduced, made us wish for the delicious moment when Mme. de Quirinodo would initiate her to the smarting discipline of the school.

This was not long delayed, for it was necessary to

overcome forthwith the young girl's resistance, who replied with regal insolence to the orders of the teachers and the Deans.

They allowed her eight days to become acclimatised, and to impress on her mind the habits and customs of the school.

During these eight days there were no public punishments, and the students, having understood that the President wished to make a big effort on the haughty temperament of Miss MacAnnay, did not reveal to the new one the means which Madame de Quirinodo had the habit of employing to chastise the rebellious.

We lived in feverish impatience. Each morning on getting up, we would ask ourselves: "Is it to day that the skirts of the impudent one will be lifted?"

The day which we were waiting for fell on the first day of the second week that the Scottish girl had spent amongst us.

On her way to classes, the teacher, Miss Elisa, made a remark concerning her hairdress arrangement according to the last Parish fashion, with a mauve ribbon, that ran through the reddish gold of her magnificent hair.

"Miss," replied Kate, looking impudently at Miss Elisa, "I beg you to leave my hair alone. It pleases me to dress my hair thus, and I shall not change it simply to please you!"

"That is to be seen," replied Miss Elisa, with a knowing smile. "For the present I shall inform the President of your impertinent reply."

She left us by ourselves and went in search of Mme. de Quirinodo.

No one in the classroom said a word; each of us felt that the big moment had arrived, and that queer things were about to happen.

The teacher was absent for only ten minutes.

When she returned, she seemed to be more satisfied than ever; we concluded that the President would not be long in coming.

Nevertheless, the lesson that lasted from eight to ten o'clock went by without Mme. de Quirinodo appearing.

As the chapel clock struck the first stroke of ten and as

we waited for the sign to leave the classroom, Miss Elisa turned towards us and said: "Young ladies, keep your seats, the President will be here in five minutes; she wishes to speak to one of you."

"At last Mme. de Quirinodo walked in, followed by the housekeeper and by six robust maids, and old Katherine, who carried beneath her arm a big oblong parcel enveloped in cloth.

She put the bundle on Miss Elisa's desk, who smiled as she questioned her with a movement of her head.

"I have all that is needed!" replied old Katherine with a knowing smile.

The servants lined up against the blackboard; Miss Elisa gave up her seat to Mme. de Quirinodo, who, more beautiful and more authoritative than ever, spoke in a clear and firm voice:

"Young ladies, one of your playmates has been guilty of a serious act of rebellion; she is a new girl, Miss MacAnnay. I cannot pass such shortcomings by, especially as her parents have given me absolute freedom to punish her for her shortcomings, which are more serious than I believed them to be. Yes, Miss MacAnnay, I shall be obliged to punish you, as it is customary here, that is to say, physically... I advise you to submit quietly, otherwise you will suffer all the more, as I shall be obliged to be doubly more severe!" While the President spoke, we turned our eyes towards Miss Kate, to see how she took all this.

The proud young girl, her head high, stared at the President with the most adorably cheeky air one could dream of.

"Yes, Miss MacAnnay, I am speaking to you, get up and come here!"

The imperious voice had its effect; without losing her arrogant and half-disgusted air, Kate left her desk, and stopped in front of the President.

"What do you mean, Madame, I cannot make out this ridiculous ceremony, at the most an attempt to frighten a child... Think, I am no longer a child, I am nineteen-years-old, and shall marry as soon as I shall have left here, which will not be long."

"You will marry, if you wish, when you leave here," said

the President, "but for the moment you are under my guardianship, and I promise you that you shall be whipped right away... do you understand now? Whipped naked, like a baby, big girl as you are!"

Kate's face during this speech is impossible to describe; fury contracted her features, and the milky complexion of her downy skin was stained by the blush of indignation.

Suffocated, she could find no words to say what she wished to say; her teeth gnashed with rage and her small fists were clenched, ready to fall on the face of the first person who would dare to approach.

It was necessary to act in such a way as to quickly bring matters to a finish, with the least possible fighting.

Madame de Quirinodo made a sign, and all the servants precipitated themselves on Miss MacAnnay, who gave a veritable roar of rage.

"Hussies, jades!" she screamed, "Let me go. Oh! It's vile, you are hurting me!"

This last exclamation was caused by the fact that the servants had nimbly tied her wrists behind her back, and pulled a little bit too hard on the strong silk cord.

And yet although her arms were immobilised Kate defended herself bravely, kicking her feet, attempting to reach the servants' bellies or shins.

They dragged her towards a heavy oak bench under the blackboard, and which was used only on rare circumstances, that is to say, when the victim was too recalcitrant.

Two maids pushed the bench on to the platform, so that the students should easily follow in all its details the scene that was to unfold itself before their eyes.

They pushed poor Kate on to the bench, and although she twisted about like an adder in the arms of those who were carrying her, she was soon forced to lie on her stomach along the bench, her hands tied to it in front of her, and her legs immobilised at the ankles by a strong leather strap. Now it was necessary to undress her. The victim being defenceless, it was an easy thing to lift up her skirts, which old Katherine spread over on her shoulders, pinning them to the corsage. The way she was standing hid from us the suggestive sight of the undoing of the drawers, but on hearing the exclamation of shame and indignation that the Scottish girl made, we were perfectly certain that old Katherine was proceeding with the untying of the said drawers. When she moved aside to show us the victim the operation had been completed, and we could satisfy our unhealthy curiosity in contemplating at our ease the naked bottom of the proud young lady.

It was a round bottom, plump, notable for the whiteness and the fineness of the skin, which is one of the most agreeable charms of beautiful red-haired women with downy skins.

In spite of the separation of the legs, in my opinion slightly exaggerated, the victim, by a supreme contraction of her muscles, managed to press together the two magnificent cheeks of her opulent posterior.

With all women who are whipped, this contraction is instinctive, as much by the wish to diminish the large surface dedicated to blows as by an ultimate sense of pudency, that strains to hide from view the secret spot of the lowest of animal functions.

While they were tying the poor girl, the housekeeper had opened the parcel and had taken from it a riding-whip, a switch with nine thongs, and a birch rod soaked in vinegar.

When the victim saw the instruments of torture she railed at the President, calling her a coward, a hussy, all the insults she could think of.

"I assure you," answered Mme. de Quirinodo with perfect composure, "that we shall make you change your mind."

She herself took the riding-whip, and her beautiful arm fell with force on to the big bottom that writhed, fell again while a shrill scream indicated that the pain was becoming acute.

The flagellation with the riding-whip must have been terrible. We could see large red stripes show on the sweet skin of the beautiful alabaster buttocks while they did not cease to writhe in an unruly dance.

The screams turned into veritable shrieks, and we were all as white as death, for to see the sight, Mme. de Quirinodo

whipping Kate, was as exciting a thing as could well be, to the future young flagellants that we all were.

If the pain had not been so horrible, it would have been comic to see the funny sight of the bottom, now shining like a big kettledrum of red copper.

Twenty-five blows with a riding-whip, it's something; well, it was Kate's share for a beginning.

The punishment must have been infinitely painful, for the poor girl jumped and writhed on the bench even though the President no longer flogged her.

Besides, Mme. de Quirinodo was short of breath, animation coloured her pale complexion, and such as she was, we were all tempted to throw ourselves at her feet, to kiss the hem of her skirt, so beautiful was she!

She gave the switches to old Katherine, ordering her not to spare the big bottom whose chubby and scarlet mien was veritably insolent.

The shrew armed herself with the switches, and the screams began again, more hoarse, more doleful.

One could hear the whistling of the rods in the air and the dull sound as they hit the flesh; one would think they were beating a carpet.

"Ah!... Ooh!... It hurts me! It hurts me!... My God! Enough!

The poor girl was tamed, the tears gushed from her beautiful eyes, her haughty pride disappeared, she became like us all when we were obliged to undergo a whipping. The same words for mercy came to her lips, childish, stammering, which hardly differentiate a young woman who is being whipped from a small child.

"Madame... I beseech you... enough... ah!... I shall die... aie! What pain!"

But it was understood that she was to undergo her torture to the bitter end.

When old Katherine put the broken rods aside, whose pieces were strewn on the ground, it was to take possession of the terrible cat.

The blood came at the first blow, and Kate supplicated, moaning mad promises... vowing to obey with servility whatever she was ordered to do.

When they stopped flogging her, all the skin of her bottom was peeled off, cut here and there, from whence drops of blood ran down her tapering thighs.

They untied her.

When she stood up she staggered as though she were drunk, carrying her hand to her eyes.

"Go and ask the President's pardon," Miss Elisa told her, pushing her.

Oh mystery and miracle of the whip, this young girl, proud and haughty, was prostrating herself at Mme. de Quirinodo's feet, without even taking the trouble to pull her drawers up, whose fine material and lace wound itself around her ankles.

Kate kissed the hem of the President's skirt, she kissed the rod that had flogged her, and skirts pinned up, her bottom naked, she stayed an hour exposed to her playmates' curiosity.

From that day on, the proud girl had been tamed.

Now that Miss MacAnnay had been initiated in the poignant delights of flagellation, she seemed to seek every opportunity to show us her plump bottom. Though a queer reversal of facts, this authoritative and vain young girl appeared to take considerable pleasure in the humiliations and torments inflicted on her by her teacher and the President. Mme. de Quirinodo, who must have cherished, in my opinion, a very exaggerated feeling of sympathy for the beautiful red-haired girl, did not, however, tire of inflicting on her, all the tortures that she invented.

Heaven knows if the imagination of that lady was fertile in vexations and tortures of all sorts; she was happy only midst tears and screams of pudency at bay. She was a veritable Marquis de Sade, for I believe she had all the vices of the celebrated erotomaniac.

Miss Kate was her favourite, and if she was in the good graces of the beautiful President, she served also as butt to the cruelty of this lady.

Like me, she was subjected to the ridiculous ordeal of the clyster, which they aggravated, by administering the enema with the aid of one of those enormous syringes used by veterinary surgeons for horses.

But the perversity of Mme. de Quirinodo did not confine itself to this scatologic whim.

She exercised on Kate nameless ill-treatments, subjecting her to the poignant torture which she would call English discipline. When Miss MacAnnay had committed a fault, the President would have her sent for, and after making her put on kid gloves, she would wet the gloves with salt water, so that the leather in shrinking, painfully imprisoned the fingers and the forearm.

With a rattan cane she would flog the poor girl's hands till she begged for mercy.

At other times she would oblige Kate to put on a very stiff corset laced with leather.

Mme. de Quirinodo would squeeze the poor girl in this appliance to the point of choking her.

"See," she would say, laughing, "how slim and fine a waist you have. It is hard to bear at first, I admit, but you will become the most slim and most elegant of these young ladies."

The poor girl would not reply, but would cry and supplicate that the odious corset be taken off.

Deaf to the wails, Mme. de Quirinodo would make her wear elegant boots with very high heels. These boots were pretty no doubt, but they had one essential fault, that of being too narrow.

The pain that one felt after a few minutes in these small shoes was horrible, shooting… it was a torment worthy of a torturer of the Inquisition.

I saw young girls thus shod shriek, literally crazy with pain, for Mme. de Quirinodo would force them to run, spurring them on with a riding-whip.

As it sometimes happened that the corset and the shoes would be imposed at one and the same time, it is easy to judge the torments that the poor little martyr underwent.

I was subjected once only to the punishment of the corset and the boots, but I assure you that I preferred the whipping with the rod and switches; that also is terribly painful but at least there is a certain sensual satisfaction.

Now that I was initiated to all that could be taught and shown me in the queer school, boredom weighed on my shoulders heavily.

I desired something novel, a public whipping, all that my imagination of a young girl perverted by the surroundings could wish for.

My hopes ended by being realised. I have already spoken in a preceding chapter of one of my play mates, Suzanne d'Alleuse.

She was a pretty girl belonging to the old nobility, who

had been sent to the reformatory to curb, if possible, her excessive temperament.

She had a love affair with a groom, and her virtue had floundered, and it was after this small scandal, quickly stifled by her family, that the amorous Suzanne had been sent to the reformatory.

As you can well imagine, it was not in these surroundings that her virtue strengthened; on the contrary, she gave herself up to pleasant vices, which playmates well versed in Greek voluptuousness took upon themselves to teach her.

Suzanne debauched us all, first of all because she was pretty and then because her agreeable talents were incredibly complaisant.

Since some time, Suzanne, who was of joyous and witty temperament, had become sad, aggressive and peevish.

We could not make out to what to attribute this changed mood, especially as she was becoming stouter.

Meanwhile, her fine and delicately oval physiogmony became coarser, her eyes had circles around them; briefly she showed symptoms of a malady which we did not yet divine the nature of.

We were not guileless, far from it, but neither were we very well informed on the mysteries of nuptials.

Nevertheless, we began to whisper between ourselves, for the teachers glanced with curiosity at poor Suzanne.

Once, during the German class, she was disrespectful towards "Fräulein". The latter, instead of whipping her on the spot, as was customary in such a case, showed on the contrary, a forbearance not consistent with her usual self, for she was a thorough horror.

She sent Suzanne to the President and even took the trouble to accompany her herself.

She returned alone, and from that day we no longer saw Suzanne, except through the panes of the infirmary.

Suzanne's illness began to alarm us. The maids joined in our talk and one of them told us in a low voice that our little playmate was going to have a baby.

A baby!

Had lightening struck me I could not have been more stupefied than I was by that revelation.

What man had crept into the fold, wearing feminine clothes? Georgette, Alice, Kate, Marguerite and myself made up the most extraordinary tales.

If we were not shy between us girls, the discovery that a man had seduced one of us made us wild.

The foreboding of some danger had us in its embrace, and the scandalous mystery weighing on the whole affair drove us into an indescribable state of enervation.

During the night I was haunted by dreams of rape and violation... the least noise made me start... my breath held back... it was infernal.

If one takes into consideration the excessive nervousness of a young eighteen-year-old girl , for I was eighteen at the time, the reader will not be surprised to hear that one day I forgot myself and raised my arm against one of the teachers.

It was on a Friday. There had been a storm all day, and the warm, sultry atmosphere, saturated with electricity, acted on my nerves, putting me into a fearful state of irritability.

It was during the physics class, and as I have said, it was a professor from the town who came for this class. I believe having said a word or two about this man in a preceding chapter.

He was about forty-five-years-old, neither handsome nor ugly, screening a sneaking look behind gold-mounted spectacles. An unfrocked priest, he was Mme. de Quirinodo's evil genius, whom had converted to the shameful cult of Satan. I found out since that he practised black magic and the Devil's mass, and seduced young girls who Mme. de Quirinodo procured for him.

The Professor was, by the way, always well behaved towards us.

His conduct never gave cause for the slightest suspicions, but we were not quite at our ease when he would look at us with his small inquisitive eyes behind his gold spectacles.

We were, as I said, that day taking our physics lesson,

the professor was teaching the class, while Miss Elisa was exercising her redoubtable surveillance over us.

All day she had irritated me with her remarks, harassing me ceaselessly, like a gadfly does a horse.

This on top of the storm had enervated me to the highest pitch, and when she apostrophed me once again during the lesson I could not prevent myself from shrugging my shoulders.—"Come here," ordered Miss Elisa, who had seen the movement.

I went up to her as I knew it would be preferable not to resist. Evidently she was going to send me to the punishment room, and I would be whipped in the evening, for they never whipped a girl in the presence of a man. As I passed by her she cried to my face:

"And try and behave yourself on the way, or I'll give you a whipping forthwith!"

This threat in front of a man unloosened my temper, and I raised my arm, without however hitting her. The movement had been quicker than my thought, but I had nevertheless stopped myself in time, crushed by the enormity of the act I was about to commit.

"Ah! This is the limit, it is the first time I have seen such a thing! You have dared raise your arm against me !"

The lesson was interrupted; the professor, his hands behind his back, contemplated the scene with a sly look.

IV

MISS ELISA SENT a student to fetch the President while breathless with fear I clutched my breast. The President was not long in coming: she walked majestically, and nodded a friendly good day to the professor who answered with a bow.

She listened to what had occurred.

"What? She did such a thing, she dared to do such a thing; Miss Elisa, bend her down and give me your rod, that I may give her a good whipping."

"Oh! Madame," I sobbed, "not here—think, in front of a man, it's infamous—flog me very hard if you wish, but not here, not here!"

"You shall certainly be whipped naked, and in the presence of your professor; I hope that in this way the shame that you will feel will be a salutary ordeal for you."

I do not even know how it happened. I was helpless to struggle, tearless to cry, voiceless to scream. In a twinkle of an eye I was shamelessly bent down beneath Miss Elisa's arm, who took good care to turn my back in the Professor's direction.

Mme. de Quirinodo's expert hands raised my skirts and slipped in between the slit of my drawers, which this time, were open drawers.

The chemise pushed up beneath the corset, my bottom blossomed out like a beautiful fruit out of its skin.

I had hardly felt all the horror of showing my bottom to the physics professor when *flip, flap, flip*, the rod made my buttocks dance with more agility than I would have desired.

Mme. de Quirinodo hit with all her strength while Miss Elisa exerted herself in presenting my bottom well tendered to the flagellating fury of the beautiful President.

While I was undergoing this painful punishment I was like a corpse. The disgrace of being whipped in front of a man was so acute that I was deprived of feeling.

Mme. de Quirinodo administered two or three dozen blows with the rod, before my screams were heard.

Then only, pain triumphed over the apathetic dumbness in which I was plunged.

I began to scream, to cry, to do all sorts of humiliating ridiculous antics, which I used to do in similar circumstances.

When wearied of beating me, or having judged the punishment sufficient, Mme. de Quirinodo made a sign to Miss Elisa to stand me up. I felt dizzy, and then my eyes glancing in the direction of the Professor whose face seemed congested, I went into a real fit of hysterics, rolling myself on the floor, heedless as to what I showed, beating the floor with my clenched fists and shrieking at the top of my voice.

I vaguely heard Mme. de Quirinodo say: "Carry her to my room and send the students to the study room; the lesson is over."

They carried me to the President's room, and I remember in a confused way the latter bending over me, making me smell the contents of a small bottle, which must have sent me into a deep slumber.

What happened while I slept I shall never know, although the events which followed gave a certain precision to my doubts.

I must have slumbered through the whole day, and when I came to myself I was alone in the room.

A shooting pain in the innermost part of my body made me understand that I had been a victim of an odious outrage.

There could no longer be any doubts, my innocence had been ravished by what worthless wretch? Following whose complicity?

At the thought of the disaster of my dishonoured flesh, I began to cry, unendingly, without either will or strength to

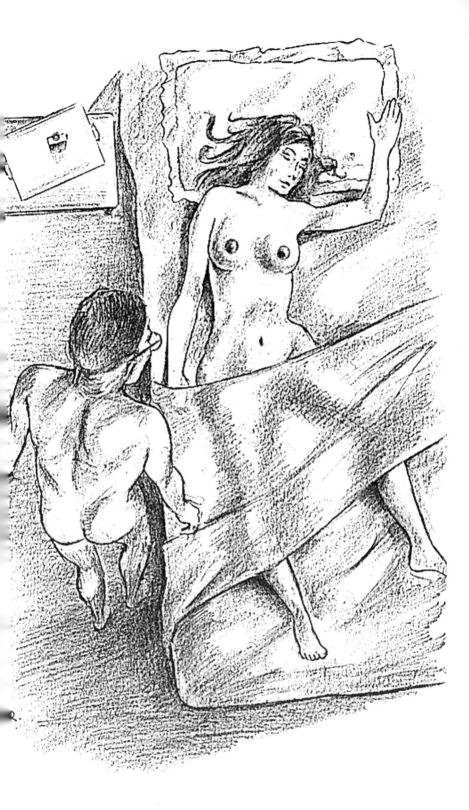

react, crushed by this last accident which polluted me, in ravishing the thing most sacred that a young girl possesses.

A conclusion is necessary to the first part of these strange and truthful memoirs.

It was the law that took upon itself to conclude the painful pages that I lived through in that hell.

At the complaint of several students, and especially former students who Mme. de Quirinodo had not had the ability to keep in her special devotion, the police made a raid, and unheard of things came to light on that which took place in the school, which had as its aim reformation of too light-headed or too wild young girls.

Suzanne, who had given birth to a baby, told all she knew, and then others followed suit, and related how they had been victims of the physics professor, who gave them lessons in the manner of doctor Pangloss.

Thus I acquired the sad conviction that the wretch had profited by my slumber to dishonour me.

V

I FOUND THE château of my parents little changed. My father was getting older every day, and my stepmother, odd to say, seemed to me pretty.

When she asked me if I had been whipped when I was at Mme. de Quirinodo's, I replied without false shame that I had indeed been whipped on many occasions.

She asked me my impressions, and told me smilingly that she would not scruple to continue to punish me in this way.

I did not reply, but in the way I smiled she clearly read that I consented.

Do not expect that I shall describe to you the floggings that I got from my stepmother. The aim I had when I started these memoirs is attained, that is to say that I wished to judge nothing, leaving to each one to infer that which he wishes according to one's morality and one's virtues.

On ending the first part of my memoirs, I had thought to commit to the readers but my memoirs of childhood, concerning my experiences and especially the punishments that I underwent in the Reformatory where my stepmother had imprisoned me.

After reflections, and I must say it, at the request of some friends to whom I read this manuscript, I decided to give a sequel to these pages and to relate the rest of my life up to the age that I now am, and that I confess, without false shame, to be thirty-years.

I am still a young and pretty woman, I can say it without false modesty, and I hope that life still has in store for me some agreeable love affairs according to my tastes.

Nevertheless, I close herewith the romance of my life, reserving to myself the pleasure of giving a sequel to this series of "slices of life," to talk in the manner of a man of letters. If however, chance grants me the good luck of living through a few pleasant and gallant scenes, according to the pure

traditions of French wit, which knows neither fetishism nor any other words in "ism", but which fully rejoices itself at the sight of the rounded forms of a laughing and beautiful girl, roguish and lackadaisical.

I had promised myself that I would not speak of the whippings that I received at the hands of my stepmother, from a feeling of modesty easily explained.

I came back from the Reformatory, a big young girl eighteen-years-old, knowing a lot of things, without, for sure, having acquired any virtues: on the contrary, having learned to submit to brute force, at the expense of my bashfulness, of my frankness and of my dignity.

I found my father's château as I had left it. The number of basset-hounds had alone increased. As regards my father, his welcome was rather cold. I forgave him, I found out since that my stepmother, that tall blonde, reserved and wicked, had completely enslaved him, and that the lack of will-power of the poor man had done the rest. Besides, I had the grief of losing him soon after my return. Grief? I do not wish to lie. My two years spent at Mme. de Quirinodo's had entirely deprived me of all affection towards him... and towards everybody.

My affective feelings were dead; but I was often caressing and amorous, but I never loved anyone, if it was not perhaps... the harsh mistress who made me bend down beneath her sceptre.

When I came back home, nothing, as I have said, was changed; the same old maid, the old gardener, and a young groom, seventeen-years-old, who certainly must have been on very intimate terms with my stepmother; but I do not wish to say anything more on this subject. My stepmother had changed little. She was the same tall blonde woman whom I had known when I had left, and a little bit of embonpoint suited her; besides she was still a young woman, being at that time hardly thirty-years-old.

When the station fly dropped me at the château, it was she who came out to meet me. An equivocal smile lighted up her usually indifferent countenance. She was pleasant, offering me

her hand to get down, and while the groom took charge of the
trunks, she herself lead me to the rooms she had got ready for me.
A large room, whose windows looked over the park, which to me
seemed very neglected, and a large dressing room adjoining.

The light-coloured curtains and wallpapers delighted
me: after the reformatory this was paradise regained.

My stepmother left me by myself to allow me to dress
myself, as the dust of the road had dirtied my blouse and my skirt.

What a feeling of happiness! I was no longer the same
girl who had left. Two-years had formed, between the girl I now
was and the kind I had been, a gulf that made me see life in a
different light.

I thought of all this as I changed my dress, and curious
to say I felt no hate whatever towards my stepmother, whose
perfidious wickedness had given me the opportunity to write
down the poignant recollections of Mme. de Quirinodo's
boarding school.

As I was making a knot in my neck-tie my stepmother
came in, after having knocked a familiar little knock at the door.

"You are already dressed, Lucette! "She sat down in an
armchair near the fireplace and pointed to a chair opposite her.

"It is a long time, child, that we have not seen each
other. You have changed, and I may say without flattering you
that you have become a very beautiful young lady."

I blushed with pleasure at the compliment. My
stepmother continued to talk without staring at me, but sending
ever now and then a glance in my direction equivocal and
knavish, but the expression of which did not displease me.

On the contrary, this hypocritical woman, artful and
perverse, excited my curiosity, and besides, at Mme. de
Quirinodo's I had seen as much.

I was therefore expecting my stepmother to question
me as to the reason of my return, that is to say, a difficult
problem, since in a way my freedom had been bought dearly
with the innocence of a virgin.

She did not speak to me outright of that scandal and
seemed to consider *that thing* of no importance.

As to me, I did not insist either, but let her question me leaving her to guide the talk, which, to say the truth, was but subtle investigation as to the transformations that discipline may have effected on my character.

With the artfulness of a cat playing with a mouse, with the reticence of a mundane and gallant abbé confessing a flighty society woman, she made inquiries concerning life there with sufficient prudence.

I felt her beat about the bush, but she did not dare make a direct allusion, and I, on my part, took a malicious pleasure in not going forward to meet her meaning.

At last she came to the facts.

"Did you ever suspect, Lucette, the reason which urged me to ask your father to send you to the boarding school?"

"Hum," I replied, lowering my eyes, "you did not like me very much!"

"Oh! I liked you well enough," replied the hypocrite, "but you were so nervous, so disobedient, so undisciplined, that it was my duty to subject you to an influence severer than mine, since you did not wish to submit to me."

"I assure you, Madame—"

"No, what I say is absolutely true—do you remember— a few weeks before your departure I had come into your room, do you remember?"

I nodded with my head. It was that day when my stepmother, thinking to surprise me defenceless in bed, had been obliged to beat a retreat in front of my energetic resolution to keep my threatened bottom free from any flogging.

"I had promised to whip you," my stepmother continued, playing with her gauze shawl, "and you had rebelled."

I still did not reply, and she went on:

"It is for that reason that I sent you to Mme. de Quirinodo's, hoping that you would there learn a lot of things as to the way that young girls can be made submissive. You must have changed since then."

"Yes," I timidly replied.

"And if sometimes, I do not believe it, but in case you

did not behave, and I consider a punishment necessary, will you submit to it now?"

My head bent down, I wriggled in my chair, the ridicule of such a cross-examination put to a young girl eighteen-years-old did not escape me.

My stepmother continued: "When I shall threaten you, let us say the word, with a *whipping*, will you be submissive?"

I was violently blushing; the tall blonde now riveted her mawkish yet domineering gaze on me.

"Go on, answer me," she said—"you must know what it is like?"

Stammering, my eyes misty, I could not manage to let out a yes.

Once again I made a sigh of assent, bending my head quickly over my bosom, and my stepmother kissed me on the forehead.

During a few days the intercourse between my stepmother and myself was as friendly as could be.

I knew that she was now certain of having me under her sway, and as all good things must be tasted slowly, she patiently waited for the psychological moment to arrive; to lift up my skirts, and make me feel the strength of her arm.

This comedy which we played at each other was so amusing, that it gave a certain piquancy to the everyday banality of giving and taking a whipping.

Since we were accomplices, she, enjoying to give, and I, enjoying to take, it was an easy matter to be on good terms with each other.

Nevertheless, I considered it more "decent" if I may use this word, that she wait for some real ground to punish me and treat me like a little girl.

In fact I was but a little girl, only a child, and my perversity did not go beyond the allurement of receiving a few lashes which gave me nervous sensations, and in spite of the smarting pain, caused a real feeling of well-being and appeasement.

My stepmother did not go beyond what is limited by a whipping, and let those young girls or young women who have not experienced the need of being whipped, or of whipping, throw the first one—if they dare.

During some weeks, even several months, nothing happened, and this patience of my stepmother's is accounted for by a grievous event which veiled the château in mourning.

My father died.

This event did not change the surface of things. He willed to my stepmother the whole of his fortune—the château and its dependencies, which however was to be mine at the death of the latter. Besides, he left me a dowry of 100,000 francs, and a sum approximately the same which I was to receive on coming of age.

I said above that I did not love my father very much, yet I cried my heart out when he died. I shall pass over this painful subject in silence, merely stating that my stepmother beneath her false tears could not help showing all the satisfaction she felt at being free, and the possessor of a large fortune and of some fine property.

Mourning suited us well; she was a pale blonde, thus dressed she appeared extremely distinguished looking; as to myself, everybody knows that black marvellously suits a pretty young girl, even though her hair is dark auburn.

Now my stepmother was all-puissant. My father had of course been an obstacle to the realisation of the projects which she had planned for me.

For indeed, punishing a big girl as they punished us at Mme. de Quirinodo's was a bit dangerous, and any hazard may have acquainted my father with that which was going on in his house.

When scandal was no longer possible, my stepmother did not trouble to hide from me the manner in which she meant to remedy my faults.

One morning, I had hardly finished my breakfast when I heard her voice calling from the stairs:

"Lucette ! Lucette, come quickly, I need you!"

I ran up the stairs four by four, and came all breathless into her room.

"See, my child," she said, "what I have bought for you."
She pointed to a large oak box on the bed.

"Open it," she went on, "I thought you as inquisitive as a cat.

I opened the box and saw: a small riding whip with a gold knob, a rod similar to the one at the reformatory, six birch switches with red velvet handles, and a girdle similar to those that are still to be seen in certain holy orders.

"It is for you," said my stepmother.

I made a wry face and then a pout at seeing this arsenal, whose copiousness was to serve to render into bright red a certain part of my body, which harmoniously distended my skirts from behind.

"At least you will not beat hard," I murmured, lowering my eyes like an innocent little child.

"That will depend on your behaviour," replied my stepmother.

"With the switches it is still bearable, but the riding whip!"

I took it in my hand and swishing it through the air, I felt a tingling all over me.

Had my stepmother ordered me to raise my skirts at that moment, I would have done so unhesitatingly.

That ceremony was postponed until the next day, and I shall remember all my life the bizarre impression caused by that whipping, inflicted on me in my room by my stepmother, whom I had formerly hated as much as anybody could be hated.

The pretext was a simple one, mere laziness on my part, and I swear that I did not expect that for this cause. I was in bed and I thought that my stepmother would prefer to administer the punishment after I was dressed, to taste the pleasure of the lifting up the skirts, which in my opinion is probably the most moving phase of the ceremony.

Several times my stepmother had made remarks on the bad habit I had of laying in bed in the morning.

A few days before she had threatened me with her finger, telling me: "You'll see what will happen to you!"

I had smiled, for I knew that which would happen.

On that morning I was voluptuously idling in a half-waking state, peopled with agreeable dreams. I was at the dressmaker's trying on a dream of a coat, extremely chic with beautiful line.

Steps on the stairs did not disquiet me as I thought that the maid was bringing me my breakfast, as she was accustomed to do, when I had not come down to the dining-room at nine o'clock.

The door opened and my stepmother walked in, carrying under her arm a birch switch which must have been left to soak during the night, for it was pliant, and smelt of that pleasant odour of damp wood which uplifts the heart of flagellants.

"You have not got up yet, lazy girl, this time you will get it, and a goodly one!"

At this I had sat up in bed, opening wide my eyes, and the rod brandished beneath my nose recalled me to the reality of things.

"Go on Lucette, turn around quickly, that I may give it to you!"

I turned on my side and my stepmother, throwing off the bedclothes, lifted up my nightdress over my shoulders, holding it with her hand, and at the same time pressing on my neck to make me bend my head.

I helped her out: "Here you are," I said, as I lay down flat on my stomach, the stomach on a pillow to raise the field of operations. "This way will be better. I'll hold my chemise," I added, laughing in my sleeve: "I shall not do it again."

I held up my nightdress myself, and turning my head I glanced over my shoulder to see the face my stepmother would make at the contemplation of my plump bottom.

She was as red as a poppy, holding the birch switch in her hand, and her gaze riveted on the globes of white flesh with their delicate pink tints.

I arched my back, spreading out the field of operations where the smarting action of the whip was to ensure, after the fashion of Mme. de Quirinodo's school, who knew how to heat a girl's bottom without the assistance of a stove!

The switch whistled through the air three times in empty space, and in spite of myself my bottom contracted, making two little dimples in each cheek. Just as in the drawings of Fragonard or of Watteau, where plump marchionesses show what I was showing to abigails acting as buffoons—but behind the half closed doors, I can assert that there were no indiscreet eyes.

At last the switch came down across my two white cheeks, and I felt the exquisite little thrill.

A few blows followed, though not hard, hardly reddening the delicate skin, and then my stepmother, throwing the bedcovers with compliance over my displayed buttocks, left without a word, assuredly more agitated than her victim.

This is what she called a whipping! I could not help

laughing: with a leap I was in front of my looking-glass, and tucking my neck like a screw I inspected the odious ravages made by the barbarous instrument.

A peachy-pink tint stained the upper part of the twin sisters; hardly a suspicion of pink on the rounded globes with their warm hue of old ivory.

Really it was not very dreadful!

How different this seemed to the floggings administered by Miss Elisa! One used to feel those for a whole week. Ah! She knew how to whip, indeed she did! My stepmother badly needed to ask her counsel in the noble art of making damsels scream while breaking down their pride.

Decidedly, if I want to be decently whipped; I must make my stepmother be equal to her mission.

How was it to be done?

The whole of the following day was delightful. My stepmother was kindness itself; and I felt that she was dying to ask me news of my glorious seat.

"Does it still pain you—there?" she asked me, touching the spot over my skirt which it moulded exactly.

"Oh! You have not been naughty!"

"They whipped you harder at Mme. de Quirinodo's?"

"Oh, yes !"

"Another time—you'll see—but you must tell me about one of your punishments there—in all its details."

As I had promised to my stepmother, I had to fulfil my promise, and related with a wealth of extraordinary detail the punishments that I had received, and those that I had seen given.

I dwelt long on the flagellation of beautiful Kate MacAnnay which have already scrupulously related in the first part of these confessions.

Then I passed on to my personal impressions, and emboldened little by little, I vindicated a punishment which two-years ago seemed to me ridiculous, indecent and barbarous.

I omitted nothing. Neither the description of the preparations, nor of the instruments employed. I described the different ways of whipping, peculiar to the Quirinodo boarding school and the personal methods of procedure of Miss Elisa, of Mme. de Quirinodo, of old Katherine, a virtuoso of beetle flogging, who could have given lessons to Emile Zola's *Gervaise*, and which the *Assomoir* contains an epic recital of the flogging she administered *coram populo* to the tall dark-haired women.

While I was speaking, my stepmother literally drank up my words. She was an unconscious flagellant who revealed herself, now that she was being instructed by her who was to act as victim.

"Then," said my stepmother, "you were whipped till the blood came?"

"I should think so!"

"How many blows?"

"That depended; with the switches up to fifty blows, a hundred as in Kate's case; with the rod up to fifty; with the crop up to twenty-five; with the beetle up to twelve, sometimes more; it all depended on the force employed."

"Have you been whipped till the blood ran?"

"Seven or eight times; my bottom peeled in several places and the blood stained my skin."

"Oh! What a horrible thing," she said, feigning horror, "you must have screamed—and did you not like it?"

"Frankly speaking no— at first it hurt a lot, especially when the switch strayed towards my delicate pinkness, but afterwards—it was like a sweet numbness as if one had drunk honey and one felt queer."

"Ah, but here," said my stepmother sighing, "I could not whip you like that, your screams would be heard."

"There is a way," I replied, for at that moment I was driven by a demon. I took my handkerchief and put it into my mouth, simulating a gag.

My stepmother understood. The hour had come. This ticklish conversation had driven us to the last limits of enervation.

If no one had been there to give me the whip, without saying a falsehood, I believe that I would have had a fit of hysterics.

Quickly my stepmother locked the door, closed the windows of her room and pulled the double curtains across them, to deaden any indiscreet noise which may have betrayed that which was about to occur.

A low divan seemed ready for the operation, and I knelt before it, my face hidden between my elbows which leaned on the divan, in a posture which raised and presented in all its amplitude the object which my stepmother's feverish hand was to denude.

The latter, while I was making ready to receive the whipping, had taken from her wardrobe a perfectly new rod which she had had bought by her maid, under the false pretext of beating some old clothes.

Knowing that the lifting up of the skirts is an infinitely delicate pleasure to the whipper, I let her do it herself, docile, passive, waiting with an exquisite thrill of anguish the first lashes of punishment that, this time I could not doubt it, would not be a laughable one. It would be given according to the rules of this art as practised at the boarding-school.

How well I knew the exquisite anguish of these preparations; the raising of the skirts tucked up over the nape, the groping hands, searching for the drawers' ribbons. I lifted my knees so as to allow my stepmother to pull down that garment over my ankles, and the chemise raised, the air bathed my buttocks, cheeky, rounded, offered in a most provocative curve. Good Heavens! I was mad.

Like at first, my stepmother contemplated my forms, and then her hand slapped my bottom, quickly, hard, which soon warmed the fine skin to my lower cheeks.

I received at least twenty slaps, and I must say that the spreading out of my bottom did not last long, as after the tenth slap I had flattened myself, contracting the twin sisters; vainly trying to diminish their amplitude.

Then my stepmother took hold of the rod and came to the second part of the programme.

She circled my waist with her arms and drew me towards her—she had seated herself next to me on the divan—and she moved one knee under my stomach, forcing me to tender my buttocks and offer them beautifully.

Then, her right arm equipped with the rod, she gave me the first lash. *Oh! la! la!* The twiglets bit into the lovely apple of my pink flesh. Truly the voluntary gag that I had employed was necessary, for after the seventh blow I shrieked as loud as I could, as in the good old times when I was a boarder. And thanks to this precaution, only hoarse and stifled sounds could be heard, and the whistling of my panting breath.

This time my stepmother was well initiated. She gave me more than I had hoped for; unable to speak I joined my begging her to stop. She went on whipping at her pleasure and when she released me from her clasp and gave me back the use of my tongue, I could only rub my hands over my inflamed bottom, and jump around the room like a child so intolerable was the smarting pain of my bottom.

During two or three days I could hardly sit down and little "aies!" quickly stifled, would make my stepmother laugh. Every morning she came to see the condition of my bruised moon, and she knew it in all its details, I can assure you.

I received two more such whippings and then—the big event came, under the disguise of a young man, my fiancé and then my husband.

VI

THAT YOUNG MAN went by the name of Guy, wore a handsome fair moustache, and knew my stepmother since long.

Where and how he had made her acquaintance I cannot say, but it was she who invited him to spend a few days at the château.

The reader will notice that I had, up to now, given little attention to young men. I never thought of them and, excepting that small and not very naughty perversity (I mean my taste for the whip) I had never thought of dreaming of a young man, poetical and sentimental; in short, possessing all the attributes of a fiancé in a novel.

I was not ignorant of certain things of life, the scandal in which I was involved was the best proof, still the thought did not immediately come to me that I was one of those young girls "with a stain", which the dowries blanched sufficiently to allow them to find a husband.

When my stepmother came to inform me that M. Guy de Montrose would perhaps be our guest for a fortnight I could not refrain a small pout of displeasure.

My stepmother noticed and said: "But how stupid you are, Lucette, on the contrary, it will be a diversion for you; you live too much alone."

It was true, I lived like a little savage, seeing no one, confiding in no one. I had no friends. My stepmother was my accomplice, she whipped me and was the instrument of pleasures, but she was not a friend; I never unburdened to her the secrets of a young girl, my thoughts.

"I shall certainly not make friends with this *young man*," I said, uttering the words "young man" with all the contempt that I felt for the strong sex.

"Phaw!" said my stepmother, "at least a comrade. Know, little one, that he plays tennis very well, and besides, it is my wish!"

"And if I did not so wish?"

"Then you know what awaits you."

"Well I do not wish!"

With the movement of her arm my stepmother drew me towards her and before I had time to say Christopher Columbus, my tucked-up skirts and my half-opened drawers revealed the plump and rounded surface, which soon began to redden beneath her slaps.

I had got what I wanted.

A few days later M. Guy de Montrose, a marquis, my dear, made a great entry into the ancient manor, where two admirable rooms had been prepared for him. I had been entrusted with the arrangement of these rooms and as I had not the least idea what pleases a young man's mind, I had accumulated books on the shelves and ash-trays and tobacco bowls in all the corners.

All the same I had taken care to flatter his poetical tastes in placing on his table a large bunch of wild flowers which I had picked in the morning, dressed in a white dress with a large straw hat, just like a little marquise of the Trianon.

The phoenix arrived at last towards mid-day. Everybody was awaiting him on the porch. It was the station fly that brought him and all his trunks.

My stepmother attended to the introductions, and while she did the honours of the château, I curiously observed the companion who was to share my existence during some time.

Tall, fair, a small conquering moustache, blue insignificant eyes, the elegance of a good tailor, such appeared to my eyes M. Guy.

He was pleasant, not very intelligent, just what was necessary; knew about horses, a few sports, and had had, I found out later, a connection with a chorus girl which had created for him a prestige amongst his friends that had made him become a bit famous.

In short, at dinner, I must have seemed to him rather stupid, and in spite of Miss this and Miss that, all I could reply was: yes or no; bending my head down like a little boarder.

That night I could have slapped myself with pleasure, at having been so stupid.

The next day during a game of tennis, things improved. Thanks to the ardour of the game I ended by feeling less savage, and asked him if he enjoyed the country, if he was not bored in this out-of-the-way château, if he lacked nothing in his rooms.

He answered my questions with perfect amiability, and when the bell rang for dinner we had already made plans for some bicycle excursions.

During all the week, my stepmother discreetly chaperoning us, we explored the countryside.

M. Guy enjoyed his stay at the château. He stayed ten, fifteen, twenty days, a month and then two.

I was quite used to him and he courted me so nicely and discreetly, that my coquettishness was delighted by it.

One day my stepmother called me and leading me into the garden, she told me outright: "I have something very important to tell you, Lucette; guess what?"

I shrugged my shoulders, arching my eyebrows, to show her that I was far from capable of guessing riddles.

"Well, my dear, M. de Montrose asks your hand in marriage. He has gone to the neighbouring village and will come back in seven or eight days to have your reply!"

"What! My hand! But I do not want to marry!"

"Don't be ridiculous, my dear; it must happen one day or another, and of course Guy is a very eligible young man for you—after that affair which, after all, had too much publicity."

And before I could put in a word, my stepmother told me in detail the story of M. de Montrose, what she knew of his fortune, of his character, *etc., etc.* She ended in assuring me that he loved me madly and was capable of committing suicide if I proved to be inhuman.

In all this business, I saw but one thing: that I had one week to think in, and asked my stepmother to allow me that much time before giving an answer. She agreed to this

During this lapse of time reserved to my meditations, when I would weigh the pros and the cons of the matter, my stepmother did not cease chanting praises about M. Guy.

He was the handsomest, the most intelligent young man on earth. He adored me to the point of madness; his only fault was not to possess money, but I was rich for two.

This consideration helped me feel attracted to M. de Montrose. His nobility was as good as mine, I could find no arguments, and before the week was out I answered my stepmother that I would do as she wished.

Now marriage showed up its good points. It was an opportunity to start a new life, and I was already happy at the thought of being a lady, and I began my trousseau.

Naturally I was to be married in white, with the crown of innocence on my head, and, in fact, in spite of my accident, I was as pure as many others whose capital is still intact.

Guy de Montrose returned at the end of the week. My stepmother told him the good news. His pleasure seemed to me sincere.

Do not expect, my readers, that I give you a description of the wedding-day; it was a fastidious ceremony, interminably long. I can recollect only an atrocious headache. My first wedding night was spent on the Côte d'Azure, from whence I went to Italy with my husband.

Guy was charming with me, and the lovely voyage that we started on overwhelmed me with joy. I was going to see lovely, poetic Italy!

We stopped at Florence. Thence, continuing our trip to Rome, we went to Naples where my husband had rented a villa on the Pausilippe. A magnificent villa buried in oleanders, palms, aloes, giant geraniums and eucalyptus.

It was a terrestrial paradise. At the foot of the hills the Bay of Naples spread out, the blue water spotted with white sails. In the distance on the horizon, Vesuvius was lightly giving out smoke, standing out in mauve against the gold of the sky.

Our honeymoon was spent in this magnificent scenery.

I was happy, I loved my husband, I loved nature, I loved everything around me. I was never as loving as at that time.

Guy lived like a lord. He was busy making a lot of money at the Exchange. He spent lavishly and I did not reproach him for it, for I was happy at being able to buy and always buy.

I would often go to the antique dealers who sold things—so improper that I could not look at them without blushing; things unearthed in the excavations at Pompeii, it appears.

I had the wish to see Pompeii, and my husband made me enter a house of ill-fame adorned with paintings.

In the evening when we were by ourselves, Guy gave me a lesson in ancient history that was very similar to the experimental methods of Dr. Pangloss.

Marriage, the new life, all this my readers must have noticed, had deviated my thoughts from that bizarre taste which had dominated me at my stepmother's.

I no longer thought of the whip, and as my husband did not appear to be bitten by this craze, everything led me to believe that the disastrous germ had been wholly extirpated from my brain.

Alas! Nature is more bizarre than one supposes, more capricious than one thinks it is; everything would have been for the best had it not appeared again under the specious form of chance, to wake the sleeping cat, to fire the powder. Here is the story.

Guy and I had gone down to the quay to see the boat off, and to see the marine life, so picturesque and sometimes so moving.

For these excursions I would be very simply dressed in dark blue tailor, because it was important not to attract the attention of the dockers and the sailors, who if drunk would not have scruples to comment on the elegance of my dress, in heaven knows what language.

It was of course apparent that I was a foreigner, but as my clothing did not excite their warmth of rancour, they saw as they stared at me, only a pretty girl, and a pretty girl in Naples is always looked at favourably.

I was stepping over a mass of cordage, and my husband, his trousers turned up over his white boots, was following me, when turning around a corner in a small alley formed by a pile of wood recently unloaded, we heard several voices quarrelling in the sharp Neapolitan dialect.

I glanced through two planks of wood, and saw, in a sort of cross road, about a dozen hooligans, fifteen- to seventeen-years-old, and two dark-haired young girls with bronzed skins, apparently companions of these gentlemen.

I am the daughter of Eve and, coquetry excepted, curiosity is not my least fault; I therefore peeped through the hole while my husband questioned me, asking what was holding my interest.

"Wait a minute," I said.

"What's the matter?"

"Wait."

He could not see as I took up all the place, and I was not disposed to give it up. Oh no! for the scene 'twas gripping, and my heart beating beneath my corsage, I already felt—I know not exactly what—indecency, which sent my blood throbbing through my temples.

The young fellows were quarrelling among themselves. The oldest, a strapping blade, handsome as Apollo, was showing some pieces of coin outspread in his hand and, in speaking terms I could not understand, to one of the young girls, a plump, pretty thing fourteen- or fifteen-years-old, who, red with anger, answered him in as loud a voice.

This girl was the pure Neapolitan type, short, sturdy, with a round face, and almond eyes shaded by dark hair, she showed the feet of a duchess in heel-trodden shoes. Her buttocks were rounded off in an ugly skirt and my eyes immediately, I know not by what presentiment, riveted on this part of the body.

It all happened rather quickly, and the scene I shall describe unfolded itself before my eyes with the rapidity of a cinematographic film.

The young hooligan slapped the girl and the latter hid her face between her elbows, like a child trying to shield itself against being slapped.

A half-circle had formed around them, laughing and making fun of the poor girl; the most fierce was the other young girl, a small, quick, dark-haired person. It was she who gave the idea of that which followed, and thus settled affairs.

As the girl who was being slapped had her back turned to parry the blows, the other girl approached her, lifted up her skirts a little from behind, and made the gesture of a beating with her hand, looking at the same time questioningly at the hooligan.

The latter, evidently, was but awaiting for this idea; let me be forgiven, he jumped on it like a dog on a bone, and in less time than it takes to tell, the girl was kneeling on the ground, and the hooligan getting astride her, sat on her neck, obliging her to kneel and bend her head down to the ground and at the same time to raise and spread out the insolent roundness of the opposite end of her body.

Beneath the thin skirt, in this excessively stretched posture, the buttocks were clearly outlined. The hooligan lifted up her skirts and her chemise. As she wore no drawers, the feminine moon, a handsome moon of bronzed and elastic flesh, appeared to my vision, right in front of my eyes, fully exposed in a posture hiding no secrets.

All this had happened very quickly, and I did not even notice my husband who had put his head next to mine to see what was going on.

He witnessed the beating, which was one of the most glorious that I ever saw. The masculine hand slapped the woman's bottom at least fifty times, giving a lovely red copper hue to the tempting buttocks.

Odd to say, during the beating the girl hardly screamed at all, passively submitting to the punishment, merely uttering a hoarse interjection every now and then.

But if she did not scream, her miserable bottom undertook to express her feelings and her sensations for her. I have seen many a beating but never, never indeed, did I see a

bottom frisk about with such agility, and dance amusingly beneath the slaps.

My husband had witnessed it all. I was in a state of inconceivable enervation. At that moment I would have given anything to be in the place of that urchin.

Breaking regretfully away from my post of observation, I had the curiosity to try to read in Guy's face the impressions he had felt at seeing the buxom girl flogged.

None! No impression was legible. At the sight of a naked bottom he had simply laughed, like any other man would have done at such a spectacle. But it was clear as day that the sight of the beating itself had not interested him in the least.

During our walk towards the tramway stop, whence we would be driven to the Pausilippe, I tried to make him tell me his impressions and feelings on this subject.

Through that conversation I acquired the certitude that my husband was not a flagellant; that the sight of the whipping seemed to him a childish banality, and that he could not understand the magic and mysterious attraction of this word.

With resentment I ascertained that my husband would never employ this form of punishment towards me, his little wife, to whom, nevertheless, nothing could give greater pleasure.

During all my honeymoon—that I would have liked to transform every now and again into a moon—reddish in colour, I was not accorded another opportunity to see or to hear any scene connected with the dangerous taste that I cherished for the whip.

I say dangerous because, later, this desire involved me in an affair which I was only freed from after paying a large sum for damages.

I did, on that occasion, but imitate Madame de Vervins, who whipped one of her servants so severely that the neighbourhood rose against her.

But those are disagreeable recollections that I do not wish to evoke.

For the moment we were back from Italy, and installed in a very smart flat in Paris that my mother-in-law had made ready during our absence.

It was in the quiet and serious quarter of Auteuil.

I was delighted to find this quiet home surrounded by leafy trees, for autumn had not yet stripped them of their leaves that blazed out in a flourish of red and yellow gold.

After the sleeping-cars, the international railway stations, the big hotels, *etc.*, I was so happy to be in my house. Now I could play at being the mistress of the house, especially as my husband, always stuck at the Bourse, left me free scope to manage the household.

We had three servants: a cook called Victoire, a fat Bordelese, dark-haired and jovial; a small fair-haired maid called Marie, a child of fourteen, who helped her in the kitchen and accompanied her on her errands, and Alice the chambermaid, a tall blonde, slim as a reed, quite pretty, and possessing, above all, the chic peculiar to abigail in a white cap, in a black dress, and in a smart white apron adorned with lace.

Alice had worked for a long time in England, at a great lady's house—Lady Dovetard—and it was she who became my evil genius, for I always needed an evil genius in my life.

I ruled as mistress over this small world, busy with the multiple obligations and the thousand-and-one duties which devolve on a young woman beginning her house-keeping.

For the first time I was living in Paris. If you remember the first part of my memoirs before being Mme. de Quirinodo's docile boarder, I had always lived in the country. Can you imagine the joy that the little country-person felt in visiting the big shops, in looking at dresses, in rummaging about amongst knick-knacks, as I inherited from my father the exquisite taste for eighteenth-century curios, whose libertine aspects pleased me immensely.

My husband, not an artist in any way, gave me full permission! Sometimes in front of a print, slightly naughty, of Watteau or Fragonard, he would smile stupidly, and our minds in this way affirmed more each day their dissimilarity.

In fact, living daily with him, now that I was married only a few years, I could no longer bear his presence.

Everything he said had the effect of irritating me,

and sometimes some violent altercations would break out between us.

Ah! The idiot! Had he known that all he had to do was to take his wife under his arm, to turn up her skirts, and to favour her with a good beating to calm her nerves, perhaps peace would have returned to the household.

But he did not know. He did not wish to open the mysterious book of my desires, to read my soul, in the depths of my deep blue eyes. And yet, Heaven knows, I was willing to let him read what I desired.

Meanwhile, fate undid the knot in a brutal way, and my freedom was bought at a price of a painful event, and which was all the more painful as I did not feel it in all sincerity, so as not to make people chatter, and was thus obliged to remain to the end in the hypocrisy of worldly customs.

My husband died in a motor accident. He had gone to one of his friends in the country, and the chauffeur, through an unfortunate turn of the wheel, had precipitated the car against a wall.

I did not love my husband, and I would be lying if I feigned pain. I did not love him; still I had never been unfaithful to him, although the opportunities were not lacking, especially lately.

I have a lot of faults, but I am loyal. I gave my word, and I kept it.

After the death of my husband, I was a rich young widow, for he left me a fortune. Many suitors came forward for the woman, for without fatuity I was very beautiful, being only twenty-five-years-old; and also, I did not ignore it, because I was rich.

I refused all these suitors. I closed my door on everybody, and I tasted, I relished in my small house at Auteuil, the happiness of being free.

At this time my stepmother, who had come to see me through these painful moments, told me that she was going to be married to a big merchant, an exporter who was to take her with him to the colonies, to Morocco.

My stepmother left; she also was still a young woman, and a horrible fate was to meet her there in a hideous death which the papers and a woman witness gave me the details of.

My husband had two sisters, one was a widow, and the other with a husband, the Commandant of a regiment of the Paris garrison.

The widow happened to die, and very naturally I took her small daughter to live with me, to act as her guardian.

This little girl was thirteen-years-old and was very pretty; she was already a little lady, with the manners of a baby, making her charming. Fair like wheat, with beautiful black eyes, she was really a lovely specimen of that delicate bibelot, complicated and perverse, which is called a little girl; especially a little girl brought up in Paris, going to a good school where they taught lots of extremely interesting things, from tennis to horsemanship.

This child was a diversion for me, and, must I say it, a talisman which shielded my virtue against the attacks of my lovers who became more and more importune since the death of my husband.

I devoted myself to my work and sent Marcelle, my niece, to the high school, as I wished her to frequent other girls of her age, to round off her edges, so that she should be rid of her timidity.

Marcelle had all sorts of good points, but on the other hand she possessed a lot of faults, of which the least were pride and temper.

This child would fly into horrible tempers over the least thing that hurt her vanity. I promised myself to punish her for this bad habit, and my readers have already guessed in what way.

It was necessary to resort to decisive measures. I knew that the little girl had never been given the whip. She had never heard of this treatment inflicted upon naughty young ladies except in children's books, due to Mme. de Segur's pen, and the beating that Sophie gets in *The Model Little Girls* seemed to her merely a bugbear destined to frighten credulous babies; she ranged the ogre in the same box.

All these stories were, for Marcelle, fairy-tales and nothing more, since reality had never furnished her an opportunity to prove the contrary.

Everybody had spoilt her at home, and the servants were at the beck and call of her whims. Her teacher herself could not manage her.

When she came to my house, she was at first very nice, very sweet, very obedient.

The new life, the control I exercised over her, all this sufficed to help her in the straight path. But one accustoms oneself to everything, and little by little the severe looks and the warnings, the scolding and the small punishments no longer had any effect. My coercive weapons were becoming blunt, the little girl was answering me cheekily; another means must be employed.

I resolved to make a big impression on Marcelle's mind, and therefore, although she had deserved being whipped at least ten times, I waited for a favourable opportunity to put to the test the good lessons that I had had in my childhood.

These were my first efforts as a whipper; I, who till then, had only humbly tendered my own bottom to the switches and the rods.

It was on a Thursday that the big scene took place. That day the pride of the little undisciplined young lady was subjected to a severe ordeal.

The two children of my sister-in-law, Germaine and André, had come to spend the day with their cousin.

Germaine was a malicious little dark-haired girl of the same age as Marcelle, and André was a pretty boy twelve-years-old.

The luncheon had been very jolly, although Marcelle, emboldened by the presence of her cousins, was more turbulent and insupportable than ever.

My hand was itching, but with the patience of a cat playing with a mouse, I waited for the opportunity.

Luncheon over, the children went down into the garden to play a game of tennis. I left them to themselves, quietly reading in my rocking-chair without troubling myself about them.

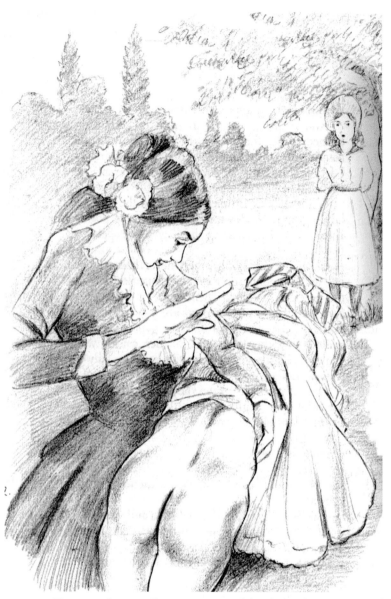

For an hour all went smoothly, but then cries of quarrelling broke out. I paid little attention to it, but the racket went on. I got up, suddenly irritated, and broke in upon them.

"Now what's the matter; you again, Marcelle?"

Marcelle, her face red with anger, angrily threw her racket down, just missing her cousin's legs.

"Marcelle, ask Germain's pardon, immediately, do you hear?

Marcelle looked at me crossly and did not reply.

Anger took hold of me, and taking her by the arm, I led her in front of her cousin.

"Ask Germaine's pardon immediately, or I shall whip you."

Marcelle tried to break loose without replying.

"I shall beat you, Marcelle; I shall do it in front of André and Germaine."

The naughty little animal turned around, and rage and shame making her lose her head, she bit my wrist.

From that minute her fate was settled, but not without a struggle, as she wriggled and scratched and screamed while I tried to lift up her skirts to reach the string of her drawers.

During this hubbub a butcher boy and an affable little maid had stopped in front of the garden railings and were admiring this picture with amused eyes.

I had to use all my strength to bend Marcelle against me, but when I had her well under my arm, she was immobilised as in a vice. With my free arm I lifted up her skirt and her starched petticoat, then pulling the strings of her drawers I broke them, and the flimsy things fell down at her heels, serving as shackles.

I lifted the chemise and revealed the pretty and dimpled little bottom, whose two cheeks contracted with shame and apprehension.

André and Germaine in front of such a sight opened wide their eyes. When they saw their cousin's naked bottom they burst out laughing, and I felt against my hip Marcelle's body tremble with rage and indignation.

While tucking up the chemise and the skirts and holding Marcelle down in her humiliating position, I was observing stealthily the play of the spectators' features.

Germaine and André had never been flogged, nor without doubt, ever seen someone flogged. And the spectacle plunged them into an inexpressible agitation, and an amused curiosity was to be read in their eyes, and their mouths gaped open in a smile of mocking scorn towards their cousin, whose vanity of a little girl trying to be a young lady was thus punished.

Marcelle was older than they were, and although she was only slightly older than Germaine, she nevertheless abused of her right of seniority, in domineering over them each time she could do so.

And they were delighted to see her thus treated like a baby while waiting for the first slap,which was to humiliate the snowy whiteness of their cousin's behind.

The first slap fell; I slapped hard and my hand made a red mark on the white and delicate skin. There were kickings of legs and Marcelle's body stiffened in an effort of all her muscles, trying to protect her bottom from the second slap.

But it was in vain. It was fated that she was to be flogged to the end.

My hand moved rapidly, slapping the elastic flesh, sowing roses where lilies had blossomed, in flaming the two dear little cheeks which expanded now, and anon contracted, depending on the blows she received.

For a first whipping Marcelle had had a thorough one. Without troubling about her cries, her sobs, her shrieks even, I slapped her bottom at least fifty times.

"Beg pardon, Marcelle."

No reply, and although her bottom was burning, I began punishing her again.

"Marcelle! Beg pardon!"

This time pain triumphed over pride, and stammering, Marcelle begged pardon, intersected with sobs.

"Better than that," and I gave her another seven or eight slaps.

"Pardon—pardon—*Oh la la!*—Pardon—I will not do—it again!"

I stood her on her feet. The pain must have been violent, for in spite of the shame she felt at being thus undressed in front of André and Germaine, she merely jumped from one foot on to another, holding her crimson bottom in both her hands.

I had to tell her to pull up her drawers, and sent her to her room on dry bread and water.

This small public exhibition did an immense amount of

good to my too turbulent niece.

In the evening, on going to see her in her room, I had expected some sort of a burst of temper, perhaps a fit of hysterics.

Nothing of the sort. Oh! Magic whip! The child was still crying, lying on her bed. The humiliation had been beyond what she had expected, and the beating she had received in front of her two cousins had broken her down, inert, after the disaster that had overtaken her now vanquished pride.

"You see, Marcelle, where your undisciplined conduct has led you. At your age don't you think it is shameful to get a whipping as I gave it to you? You can be sure that your cousins saw something, and they will not fail to tell everybody that they saw your naked bottom. For a big girl, thirteen-years-old, a nice thing, is it not! Now that you have tested this punishment which you had already deserved a good many times, but which I had not made up my mind to give you, as I considered you too big, now that you have tasted a beating, I must warn you that I shall not hesitate to punish you thus again. Each time that you will deserve it, I shall raise your dress and give you a beating. It is up to you, Marcelle, to be well-behaved and obedient, not to reply crossly, not to tell falsehoods; in short, to act in every way like a good little girl which you are at bottom."

During all this address Marcelle, still lying flat on her stomach on the bed, did not cease crying. She hid her face between her elbows in order not to show her face reddened by shame.

"Come and ask my pardon, to show that you are not vindictive."

I had to take the poor child in my arms ! Then taking her on my knees, I kissed her fair locks, comforting her as best I could, for the beating had literally afflicted her.

VII

L ITTLE BY LITTLE, under my caresses and also at the promise that I would not have recourse to this punishment if she always was well behaved, Marcelle was comforted, and kissed me sweetly, promising me not to be naughty any more.

"I shall be good, I promise you, aunt, but please, please do not invite Germaine and André on Sunday—not so soon.

Evidently she was ashamed, and at the idea alone of seeing the witnesses of her humiliating punishment, she blushed up to the ears.

"If you are good Marcelle, I shall not invite your cousins on Sunday," I replied, to soothe her, for already her beautiful eyes widened fearfully at this possibility.

During all the week Marcelle was the most charming little girl one could dream of. She learned her lessons well, studied her home-work, and came home from school with good marks.

The maid-servant could hardly recognise her. The little demon had become an angel. As the servants had been absent the day of the famous beating and as I had kept the secret at Marcelle's beseeching request, the maid could not know of the remedy withal so simple, that I had employed to curb that restive nature.

During one month all went well, but then discipline was relaxed, the remembrance of the punishment was effaced in Marcelle's memory, and she became as increasingly intolerable as before.

I did not threaten her with another beating; it is not my way.

In fact, in repeating too often: "You shall be whipped; take care or I shall pull up your skirts; you know what you will get; don't make me lose my temper or else, *etc.*" the child ends in becoming accustomed to this perspective. It knows that being the weaker, inevitably the thing will happen some time or other, and it resigns itself to the inevitable.

When if you take the child to give her a whipping, she is nowise surprised, all the moral effect of the punishment is destroyed, and in my opinion the punishment is useless.

The moral effect, I owe the psychology of this to Mme. de Quirinodo and Miss Elisa, lies in the flagellation. The shame, the deep feeling of humiliation, the unquestionable disgrace received in the presence of witnesses, there lies the real coercive means of this mode of punishment. The pain caused by the hand, by the rod, or by the switches, has too little effect on the victim; to such a degree, that they would a hundred times prefer to receive twice as many blows on the shoulders or on the hands than on their fully denuded bottoms, according to the good old ways of doing it.

The second whipping was inflicted on Marcelle without her in the least expecting it.

She received it in the presence of my maid who seemed to take an extraordinary pleasure at this sight.

In a twinkle of an eye Marcelle's skirts were tucked up, her drawers taken off and her bottom, from the most delicate pink, became a warm red.

Like as at first, she jumped and screamed, while holding her bottom in both her hands.

It was Alice, the maid, who put on her drawers. She took all the time necessary to do so, and as I observed her I could but ascertain the agitation which this small scene had thrown her in.

"Hullo, Hullo," I thought to myself, "here is a young lady who must have tasted the whip, and who does not seem to have unpleasant recollections of it.

I sent Marcelle to bed, as after a whipping I would send the child to bed to allow her to meditate on her faults, and I sat

by myself in my arm chair, musing at the queer agitation that had over taken the pretty maidservant during the whipping.

She was, as I have said in a preceding chapter, a tall slim girl, well built, with a vivacious look on her face. Up to now she had given me no cause for complaint; on the contrary she appeared to feel a deep affection for me.

None of the small requests which ladies usually ask of their maids seemed to displease her. My nudity, on the contrary, had attracted her. She liked to massage me, to rub me down after my bath, to dress my hair, *etc.*, and she would always repeat: "How beautiful Madame is; what a beautiful skin Madame has, Madame has a lovely waist," and so forth.

I was not embarrassed by her, and would ask her to do things for me that I would never have asked of another maid; she was something like a friend for me.

One morning I had asked her to give me an enema. In this I follow the old method, that is to say, I abolish the ridiculous bulky apparatus, and use a pretty little squirt in silver.

The only fault of this instrument is that it necessitates a witness. I asked of Alice the services that the Duchess of Bourgogne asked of Nanon, if one believes Saint-Simon. Alice unhesitatingly complied, and used such skill and complaisance in the operation that I clearly saw the pleasure she had in attending upon me.

The emotions that she felt while I was beating my niece enlightened me as regards my maid's character, and I resolved to observe her, while at the same time to become less familiar with her.

But the Devil disposes—on this occasion the whip and this trite pretext was the cause of certain things happening which the reader must not expect to find here.

It was the third whipping that I gave to Marcelle that led to the talk on the subject.

I had whipped Marcelle in Alice's presence, and this time, with switches, that had made stripes on her bottom, some twenty times.

My niece had gone up to her room to cry, to writhe at her ease, and I was alone with Alice, who was as red in the face as on the first occurrence.

She was busy sewing a dress-gown for me, and while working, a piece of thread between her teeth, she sighed and turned around, as one wishing to start a conversation, but who dares not.

"This is insufferable," I said, "and if it goes on I believe that I shall be obliged to whip her till the time she marries."

"Madame will do well to do so," replied Alice.

"She is, however, beginning to be too old, and I hesitate to treat her like a baby."

"Oh Madame! One is never too old to get a

whipping; I assure you that there is nothing like it to bend an intractable character."

"You know something about it then, Alice?"

Alice blushed, bent her head over her work, and did not reply.

"I think perhaps that you have been whipped more than once when you were little," I said.

"Oh!—And very often!"

It was my turn to blush, but I continued my inquiry:

"In any case it can only do good; a big person often needs to be whipped like a child," I said.

"That is my opinion too, Madame."

"It appears," I went on, "that in Russia the great society ladies do not hesitate to whip their maids when the latter deserve it. I know of several stories on this subject, and absolutely truthful, but it seems to me a little bizarre—and—what would you say—if for instance—for some neglect in your duties I should propose to give you a whipping?"

Alice lowered her eyes and replied: "I would say Madame is right if I had deserved it."

Can one be so stupid. For a week I could think only of that conversation which I had had with my maid.

I had but one desire in my brain: give Alice a whipping, lift up Alice's skirts, slap Alice's bottom!

To say the truth, although I was convinced that Alice would be only too pleased I dared not to do it. Thinking it over calmly it seemed to me ridiculous. To beat a child, even a young girl, can be accounted for by the difference in age of the one who gives the whipping and the one who receives it. But to whip a big young woman twenty-six or twenty-seven-years-old, above all a servant, it seemed to me rather puerile, as the moral pretext, the object in punishing, which indeed is the real pretext and the most agreeable attraction of flagellation, could not be accounted for in this case.

To whip Alice, who was a woman as old as I, implied a great deal of complaisance on her part.

But I did not like to give a whipping, when I knew how willing my victim was to receive it. If there is any pleasure in whipping, not counting the aesthetic pleasure of the beauty of the designated place, it is to feel against one's body a lovely body distracted with fear and with pain, whose nerves are all under tension, and who struggles to the last limit to keep as a last rampart, the drawers, the last defender of pudicity at bay.

All the delight of the whipper lies in hearing the sweet music of the supplications, the "pardon," the "I shall never do it again."

All the pleasure lies in the charming picture. The poor child, on her knees with hands joined together, the skirts tucked up, showing the lace of her drawers, and begging with sobs in her voice to be spared this time; the shame of showing her bottom to a third party who chuckles while waiting for the curtain to go up.

Hence, in whipping Alice, nothing of all this could tempt me; I would have the leisure to beat the docile bottom of a big girl, possessing a rather stupid form of perversity.

And yet it happened.

Alice, however, was so provoking in this occurrence that everybody would have acted like I did.

I can still remember this scene in all its details, moreover it is not so far back that I should forget.

It was on an afternoon of sultry heat, of enervating heat, when the atmosphere is saturated with electricity, when women's nerves tingle at the slightest sensations, and when the leaves of the trees are immobile and heavy.

I had sent Marcelle to her aunt's to spend the day with her cousins, and was alone, lying on a divan, dressed only in a black kimono embroidered with mauve flowers.

I was reading; what book? It was, I believe, a novel by Andréa de Nerciat, and this book was certainly not one to calm me.

Downstairs I could hear the plates and dishes. It was insupportable. I threw my book across the room and called Alice!

"Here I am Madame !"

My maid knocked at the door and without waiting for my reply, came in.

"What does Madame wish?"

"What I wish—what I wish—less noise; you appear to be doing it purposely; I sent Marcelle away not to be pestered by her, but I believe that you substitute her to advantage."

"But, Madame—"

"Ah! no! no! don't begin your jeremiads; I know what you are going to say—were it Marcelle, I would know how to quiet her."

Alice lowered her eyes and sent me a look that I pretended I did not understand.

"Yes, I assure you that Marcelle would have been whipped more than an hour ago, and well!"

"No; there," I said, "busy yourself in ranging the linen and mark what there is on this note book."

Alice began, and while working she at the same time acted coquettishly, taxing her ingenuity to find acted poses, to make faces, pulling out the tip of her pink tongue while laying out the drawers, and marking them down on the washer-woman's note-book.

I, as is easily imaginable, did not miss one of her attitudes, and my eyes would light up, especially when the flexible and graceful girl would bend in two, outlining beneath her black skirt, prominences of flesh which nature had agreeably modelled. Well defined, narrowly imprisoned in her skirts, the twin sisters fascinated me, and already I felt crazy itchiness in my hand to scratch, to slap, to whip.

I had got up, and while she still bent down, seemingly busy with her work, Alice appeared to pay no attention to me, and approaching her I put one arm around her waist, and threatened her with the other, saying: "Do you know, my dear, that you are well placed—"

Alice did not get up, but her lovely eyes met mine, and I clearly read what she wished.

"If I so wished I could give you a good little beating;

you are in my power. What would you say if I gave you a good little punishment to indemnify myself and to punish you?"

"Oh! Madame well knows."

"What?"

"That—I would say nothing."

"Well it is splendid then. You will get it, and well."

An ottoman near us hastened and favoured a fall, the most providential in the world.

Alice fell on her nose, pushed adroitly by me, and lay on her stomach leaning on the ottoman.

I did not lose time in talk; my febrile hands hastened to peel the beautiful fruit, to denude the tempting bottom of this big body.

She herself yielded with wonderful spirit; she got up a wee bit to allow the lifting up of her skirts, as her thighs leaning against the ottoman's edges prevented her from lifting them higher than her calves, which already showed in brown silk stockings, the colour of her boots.

My maid was elegant and I was capable of ascertaining it, when, the skirts raised and pinned to the shoulders, I saw the lower part of her body still modestly screened by a delightful pair of little drawers, drawers of a little girl almost, moulding the contours of her buttocks, and showing a little bit of pink flesh beneath a trimming of lace, which just covered the depression where the buttocks met the thighs.

I tried to separate the slit of the drawers, but Alice's bottom, round, firm and exquisitely curved, and standing out very much in relief by the posture she was in, would not show out of its envelope.

It was necessary to take off her drawers, and at last, at last, for I could no longer bear the flagellating fury, the lovely moon whiter-than-white ermine, appeared in front of my delighted eyes, like a large cream-coloured pearl in a casket of lovely underclothing.

My impatient hand immediately came into contact with the satiny skin.

Clack! Clack! Clack! Count if you so wish, the beating began, and I hit with all the strength of my arm.

On the big contracted cheeks my hand made bright red marks!

Clack! Clack! Clack! Pink blended with the lily whiteness, and Alice's bottom now leaping beneath the blows took on a lovely hue of "strawberry cream," most appetising in effect.

Clack! Clack! Clack! "There my dear, that's one for you, and another—and another. Did you make me wild a minute ago? What of this one, and that one. *Thwack! Thwack!* The beating is for big naughty girls. *Clack! Clack!* You can wriggle your big moon Miss, but you will not prevent it getting its due."

It was a Homeric whipping!

Panting, breathless, I dropped into my armchair.

In a sort of dizziness I saw Alice get up, pull up her drawers quickly, and going to the window carefully draw the double curtains across them.

An instant later the tall fair wheedling girl was beside me.

Later, my head heavy and my heart filled with disgust, remorse came to assail me. I could but say my *mea culpa*, paltry remedy. I had, nevertheless, the courage to send Alice away, whom a minute of aberration on my part had rendered despotic to excess. There could be one mistress only in my house, and I meant to be that one.

My intrigue with Alice resulted in my sending her away, and then in calming me a little.

It seemed to me that I had been cured of the mania of whipping, and I was truly happy, because this little girl's game seemed to me sometimes, after reflection, of distressing puerility.

I thought of marrying again.

But being rich, I wanted to make a love-marriage, and bring as my wedding gift, since I lacked virgin innocence, at least a little heart that had never throbbed for any one.

I resolved to go a little into society, and grant myself some mundane diversions.

I feared solitude, and I considered it, with good reason, the mother of all evils.

Evenings spent with friends took up my time; I no longer was taken up by Marcelle, whom I had sent to board with an English tutor at Brighton.

In this boarding-house, a very select one, corporal punishment flourished, and as I found out later, my pretty niece more than once experienced the taste of the whip, as I myself had done when a young girl.

I had accustomed my niece to this punishment and she must not have been very much surprised when Miss Glady, her teacher bent her down to whip her.

At this time a horrible event occurred which I will relate.

One fine morning while I was lying in bed late in the morning, happy to idly lie at my ease in my large comfy bed, my maid brought me the morning papers as well as some hot chocolate, steaming in a porcelain cup.

While letting it cool a bit, I opened my papers and was immediately struck by a big title which spread over the whole of the top of one page:

REVOLT AT CASABLANCA

The tribes mutiny—Europeans massacred.

Casablanca! That was the city where my stepmother and her husband lived. Anxiety gripped me, and I devoured the short news, too short, alas, as no particulars had yet arrived of the frightful drama which must have been enacted there.

One knew, in short, that the tribes that had revolted had entered the city, and had massacred the whole of the Jewish quarter, after having subjected the women and the young girls to nameless outrages.

Finally, in the European colony, two women had been seized by the rebels, and several men employed in the customs, and massacred after being subjected to the most atrocious tortures.

The names of the two prisoners were not given, but the following day, I could no longer doubt but that my stepmother had been one of the two.

During a month I was without any other information; then, one afternoon, as I was getting ready to go to skate, my maid came to say that a lady wished to see me on urgent business.

Slightly annoyed by this delay, I told the maid to show the visitor into the parlour, and gloved as I was, to let her see that I was on the point of going out, I came down to see her.

As I came into the parlour the visitor got up. She was a small, plump person, simply dressed with good taste. She must have been thirty- to thirty-five-years-old and her face quite pretty, which was, however, streaked by a pink scar of some old wound, as a sword cut.

"Madame, pardon me, I am Madame Carlotti, and my husband is a commercial agent. I have come from Casablanca, and must hand this package over to you."

She gave me a box containing my stepmother's wedding-ring.

I have already said previously how little I cared for my stepmother, yet in front of the brutal facts, I felt tears run down my cheeks.

"Good God! Good God!" I murmured, "What a horrible end!"

"Oh! Madame!"

"You were there, you witnessed what happened?—Tell me, the rebels tortured her, perhaps they—?"

"The most abominable things you can think of, your stepmother underwent, and in this line, the Moroccans defy the wildest imagination."

"Can you relate me the facts?"

"The fact, Madame, is that the details are somewhat scabrous."

"Go on, please, I am not a young girl, and between two women there is no need to blush."

"I must tell you, Madame, that I met Madame

Labardane, that was your stepmother's name, there in Casablanca, where she lived in a large Spanish house, separated from ours by a party wall."

"The revolt broke out on a market-day. The rebels, divided into four bands, rushed to the city entrances and while a thousand of them destroyed the Jewish quarter, some hundreds of the fiercest of them penetrated the European quarter."

"M. Labardane was killed almost immediately, without being able to use his revolver. My husband was also massacred and I owed it to the complicity of an old devoted negress, that I managed to hide myself in a small forgotten room, which was ventilated by a fissure in the wall and which overlooked my neighbour's garden."

"Although half-dead with fear, I still had, impelled by curiosity, the courage to peep through this fissure, from where I could see all the garden and some of the rooms of the ground floor."

"The noise of the guns was infernal, to which was added the yells of the rebels. They were already in the garden. Then I saw some fifteen of them enter the house, while the others riddled the dazzling whiteness of the walls with shots.

"I could hear in the house the noise of overturned furniture, and then the distinct report of a revolver. A shrill female shriek, followed by several more, was heard above the tumult of the assault.

"The Moroccans came back into the garden, which the native women and children were invading, at the same time uttering strident cries of *youh*, *youh*.

"Suddenly, amongst the bandits, I perceived a white skirt, a white blouse, a fair head. She was a European, I recognised Madame Labardane.

"She was still wearing the tennis dress that I had seen her in that very morning. She was struggling, trying to escape from her warders, who were laughing at her efforts, well-knowing that the European could not escape them.

"As soon as she appeared, the *youh-youh's* of the women redoubled; a demoniac circle of shrews, young women and

young girls, surrounded the poor woman who, distracted, looked at these devils escaped from hell, with the eyes of a deer run to earth."

"The Moroccan women seized their prey, and I witnessed, sobbing, with hands clenched in impotent fury, the horrible and shameful torture inflicted on Madame Labardane."

"Shameful because they tucked up her skirts like a little girl; horrible because the blood soon ran down the stockings and the white shoes of the poor woman."

"She was whipped?" I interrupted, "tell me everything."

"Yes, whipped, by the shrews. One of them bent her down and taking hold of the poor woman by the wrists lifted her on to her back, the stomach on her kidneys, thus holding her victim in the right posture. In this way Madame Labardane involuntarily tendered her buttocks, for I am ashamed to have to say it, it was on this part of her body that the oleander switches, with which the harpies had armed themselves, vented their fury on.

"It was, Madame, the first time in my life that I saw a woman, and above all a compatriot, in such a humiliating situation for our sex. The *thing*, that is, that part of her body, you know what I mean, on which the punishment was inflicted, was large and white at first. I say at first, for it soon began to redden beneath the blows, and then to bleed beneath the violence of the lashes…"

"When the blood began to run down her legs, Madame Labardane fainted. I could see that by her white face, from which the blood had receded, which fell on her shoulders.

"This did not stop the shrews' fury; the flagellation was interrupted, and then the women rushed on the victim, stretched out inert on the ground, and tore off all her clothes till she was stark naked.

"The tortures went on. They burned the tips of her breasts, thus drawing her out of her swoon."

"Then an abominable scene was enacted. The men rushed upon her, and that which occurred is unspeakable."

"Under the violence of the most revolting outrages the victim again fainted."

"This atrocious scene lasted an hour. On the horizon I could see the Jewish quarter burn, and from all sides the shrieks of men being butchered rang out, and the shrill cries of women who were being violated."

The visitor had ceased to talk. Deadly pale, I had listened to the terrifying recital of this frightful end.

I could not imagine such horrors, and the abominable torture that my stepmother had under gone before dying, made me feel ashamed.

Thus, I was capable of amusing myself in such a barbarous game!

But you will say, there is flagellation and flagellation, and the mother who whips a small unruly child cannot be taxed with cruelty.

It is quite true.

Nevertheless, each time that my thoughts reverted to my taste for the whip, I could not prevent myself from again seeing the distressing picture that Madame Carlotti had depicted to me.

I believe that this picture was a salutary one for me, because since that day I was much less tormented by the desire to whip anyone.

At the very least if I bought wisdom, I was from that time sure that I would no longer relapse into habits, which may in the end not have remained innocent.

These are the last pages of my confessions. They have, in my opinion, but the merit of being truthful, and of revealing a little of the straying of the soul, which young women and girls do not in general easily reveal.

How specious is the attitude of women often, and to take out one instance in the subject which here interests us, how often did I see young ladies who loudly cried out in public against the immorality and the brutality of corporal punishments, and who still felt beneath their skirts the warmth of a recent little whipping which they received not without pleasure. How often did I see beautiful and good women accuse this thing as ridiculous and childish, who that very morning had wielded with their lovely white arms the classic rod, to the detriment of the bottoms at their mercy.

But I am also of the opinion that it is not always good to be frank. Truth in all its nakedness would be hustled to prison, and to be sure, far better to keep secret, the turpitude we are not masters of, rather than spread them out in broad daylight.

If I have frankly confessed things in these pages it is because I do not have any sins on my conscience. That never hurt anyone, and my seat alone could complain of a punishment which it did not always find pleasant.

Flagellation is too big a word with which to designate that thing, and I repeat that it is improper to thus designate the punishments that a pretty mother inflicts on her little devils, or a school teacher administers to very turbulent young ladies.

I said in the preceding pages that my heart, still young—I was only twenty-eight-years-old—aspired towards love.

On a sea-coast, in an idyllic and sentimental landscape, and in a romantic background, which many would have thought rococo, I met my ideal, he whom I had so long waited for.

Do not expect a description of his beautiful eyes and of his dark moustache, the hour of confidences will no longer strike, for my love is for myself alone; it is a possession that I do not wish to lessen by giving up to the public. For, it is not true that one must keep for oneself the knowledge of happiness, when one such happiness is acquired.

Day blessed by us. We mused together as we looked over the sea spread out at our feet like a mantle of dark velvet. It was evening. He encircled my waist with his arm, bent me towards him and his lips sought my lips, which I did not refuse him.

Trembling with emotion and tenderness I felt my heart swell with a joy so pure that the beautiful verses of Pierre de Ronsard came to my memory.

A HISTORY OF THE ROD

THIS FAMOUS book was first published in 1865, at the apogee of the Victorian era. Its full title—*A History of the Rod in All Countries, from the Earliest Period to the Present Time* proclaimed its scope: and to this day it remains the largest single volume ever devoted to a comprehensive history of Flagellation.

In its own day it inhabited that eerie borderland between "medical" and "risqué", inclining rather more towards the latter. This was hardly surprising since its real author was a notable Victorian writer of flagellant fiction. To give *A History of the Rod* a measure of respectability, he adopted the pen-name of a clergyman (who in Victorian eyes could do no wrong).

The book is an astounding *tour-de-force* of flagellant history, from Biblical times, through the High Mediæval period, to the "present day" of the author's own era, when birch-rod, strap and cane were still very much in use around the world, and especially in Britain.

This AKS Books hardback edition is faithful to the original in every detail, including the illustrations.

£40.00

THE WAND OF VENUS
The High History of the Birch Rod

A DAZZLING and erudite compendium of birchen lore, compiled from a huge variety of expert sources from classical times to the present day.

It includes histories, anecdotes, eulogies, factual accounts, recommended procedures and other Arcana of the Rod, intriguingly assembled and beautifully presented with over 80 rare and original illustrations.

£25.00

THE SONG OF THE CANE

THE RATTAN CANE is the most painful of all instruments of punishment. It stings, leaves marks and evokes noisy responses; and nobody who has ever been disciplined by one will ever forget the experience. From quite another point of view, a cane is light, long-lasting, and a sensuous delight to use. Its accuracy is phenomenal: it is astonishingly economical of effort; and makes a music like no other implement. *The Song of the Cane* is an anthology of writing—fiction, poetry and factual accounts—carefully selected to provide the broadest possible view of this most dreaded of all implements of correction. Edited by Jacqueline Ophir.

£15.00

THE SATURDAY AFTERNOON DETENTION

'FOR ONCE, I was disappointed not to see a cane lying on her desk, as it would've meant that Lucinda was wrong about our crimes being reported for Mrs. Vincent's rigorous attention. After the Headmistress, it was Miss Cartwright's cane that all the girls feared most, but even an immediate thrashing from her would be preferable to the Saturday detention that was now on the cards.'

Angela Richards recollects her very personal experiences of attending a Girls' Boarding School in the early 1960s, sensitively describing her fears and the painful events which unfold on the day that she and her two best friends had to report to the Headmistress's study for a *Saturday Afternoon Detention*.

£15.00

SENT FOR SIX OF THE BEST

IN this sequel to *The Saturday Afternoon Detention*, Angela has been caught smoking in the Fourth Form washroom by bossy-boots prefect, Amanda Wilkinson. Last term, the Headmistress had decreed that if Angela, Nicola or Caroline were caught smoking again they were to be sent to either her, or Miss Cartwright for six of the best! Angela pleaded with Amanda to take her to the Duty Mistress to be punished, as she knew that if she escorted her to Miss Mitchell, her Form Mistress, she was sure to refer her to Crusty Cartwright, the irascible Deputy Headmistress for six of the best!

£15.00

THE SCHOOL RECORD

'"BEND OVER your chair," she instructed.
Remembering how Madame always seemed able to make it sting more than most of the other mistresses, even though she never raised the cane any higher, I did as directed. With my back to the rest of the class and gripping the flat, latticed seat in readiness, I looked down knowing it'd be virtually impossible to sit there through the rest of the lesson…'

Set in a strict Girls' Boarding School during the mid-1960s, you can almost hear the sound of chalk squeaking against the blackboard and the swish of the mistresses' canes! Now in the Fifth Form and just sixteen, Angela and her friends giggle and painfully wriggle through the last week of term before the Easter hols. Caroline first mentioned it at lunchtime as a joke, but Barbara Nicholls decided to ask Miss Robertson whether it had ever happened before. Angela is faced with a terrible dilemma… should she attempt the 'School Record'?

£15.00

CHÂTEAU SOUMISSION

Château Soumission is the stunning second book from the author of *The Queen of the Grove*; it includes two full-length novellas. *Château Soumission* is the ultimate "closed world", where Ladies rule, Domestics serve and the Rod is paramount... The second story is *Miss Beauchamp's Reward*: "For years she had served Our Lady of the Rod faithfully and in her own way—without once taking an active rôle. But now her time had come..."

£20.00

THE LOST BREECHES

When Pepin leaves home to seek his fortune things go badly wrong almost immediately. Within a few hours he has received the spanking of his life from an angry inkeeper's wife—and has lost his breeches into the bargain. His sole wish thereafter is to retrieve them. *The Lost Breeches* follows his unhappy odyssey as he pursues the missing garment—a journey all too frequently interspersed with the use of the Rod upon Pepin's person by the lady he has most recently annoyed: and there is no shortage of these. A delightful fairy tale illustrated by Curtus with 33 original plates.

£25.00

ACROSS MY LADY'S KNEE

When three teenage daughters of the 21st-century *belle-monde* each decide to acquire a pageboy as the latest fashion accessory, life changes drastically for the youths most closely concerned. Well-fed, well-housed and (particularly) well-dressed, the three pageboys are nevertheless also extremely well-disciplined, subject to frequent and humiliating corporal punishment at their young mistresses' whims. What follows over the next eighteen months is a prolonged—and profound—learning experience for all concerned. With 13 original plates by Curtus.

£25.00

A PERFECT MISTRESS

Jacqueline Ophir's latest full-length novel, partly a work of imagination and part autobiographical, tells the story of Miss Leah B—, who, while still in her early twenties, is obliged—by Fate, as it seems—to confront the reality of her inclinations when she disciplines a rowdy youth in the street. Soon afterwards she receives a letter from a distraught mother, asking for help of a similar nature—and so begins an extraordinary career as *A Perfect Mistress*. An exquisitely written work by the Editor of *The Governess* journal, gorgeously illustrated throughout by Sardax with several full-size watercolour plates and a large number of sensitive motifs.

£25.00

LINTON ABBEY

WHEN WILLIAM was sent to join his cousin Lucy at her mixed boarding school, he had no idea what was in store for him.

What was in store for him was the same thing Linton Abbey
School provided in full measure for all its boy (but never girl) pupils.

The Hairbrush. The Slipper. And the Cane.

Always on the bare bottom, and nearly always in front of the girls.
Then William and his friends rebelled…With six original plates by Curtus.

£15.00

IN FRONT OF THE GIRLS

THIS CHARMING and provocative collection, by the author of *Linton
Abbey*, is devoted to exploring the proposition that for a male to be
punished in the presence of—or by—the opposite sex of the same age is
perhaps the ultimate mortification. Short stories and poems of rare quality
and vivid imagination, illustrated throughout with full-page plates by
Sardax, make *In Front of the Girls* Miss Blackwood's most exciting and
accomplished work to date.

£15.00

SWEET RETRIBUTION

A CHARMING COLLECTION of essays and poems, originally
intended for *The Governess*, but never published in that Journal for reasons
of apace alone.

This constantly popular selection includes: *The Nun's Story;* a
terrifyingly true tale of how the sisters in a Breton convent punished the girls;
Community Care; in the not too distant future, women rule Society and the
Rod is back—with a vengeance! *Singapore Sting;* a young teenager steals a
brass plaque, but is found out—for an English girl the punishment is
extremely severe!

£10.00

THE KISS OF THE WHIP

THIS comprehensive and fully illustrated study of corporal punishment
was first published in 1961 when, 13 years after its abolition, there was a
public clamour to restore flogging to the penal code.

Chapters cover religious flagellation; superstition and
persecution; wife-beating and parental punishments; 'educational'
flogging in fact and fiction; flogging in the armed forces; judicial
flogging; flagellation in brothels; the whipping of male and female
servants; sadism and masochism; and the physical, sexual, and
psychological effects of whipping.

£15.00

THE ART OF DISCIPLINE
A Pictorial History of the Smacked Bottom

NEARLY 600 exquisite images from the golden age of disciplinary illustration—including more than 60 from Louis Malteste, over 40 from G. Topfer and more than 30 from Jim Black—plus dozens of drawings by Beloti, Dagy, Hegener, Herric, Milewski, Soulier, Wigead, and many other artists.

Entire classic collections such as 'Three Painful Years', 'Frenzies', 'Flora en Pension', 'A Dominant Mistress', 'Récits Piquants', &c. Hundreds of unattributed drawings covering subjects such as School, Domestic Discipline, Postures, The Weaker Sex, Judicial Punishments, and many others.

There has never been a picture book like it!

£40.00

THE ART OF DISCIPLINE
Volume Two

AT THE TIME it was produced, *The Art of Discipline* was, without a doubt, the greatest single source of disciplinary art ever published between hard covers.

The original volume could not, and did not, claim to be totally comprehensive in its assembly of images and now, this second volume clearly surpasses its highly distinguished predecessor! Comprising 40 per cent more images—820 instead of 570, *The Art of Discipline Volume Two* also contains 16 full colour plates.

Divided into three parts, 'Artists and Collections' depicts the work of the most talented artists through the ages, including many still active today. 'Personalities' is sub-divided into sections featuring 'The Dominant Female'; 'The Dominant Male'; 'The Schoolmaster'; and 'Judicial Punishment'. 'A Miscellany' includes disciplinary scenarios in commercial advertisements, seaside postcards, "what-the-butler-saw" stereo viewing machines, films and TV, comics and cartoons, plus vintage photographs and a selection of spanking machines!

The most comprehensive collection ever assembled!

£50.00

FOR A FULL CATALOGUE OF AKS BOOKS WRITE TO:

PO Box 39, Bexhill-on-Sea, East Sussex, TN40 1WR

Telephone & Fax: 44 (0) 1424 733819

Website: www.aks-books.co.uk